THE POSTMASTER'S SON

A NOVEL

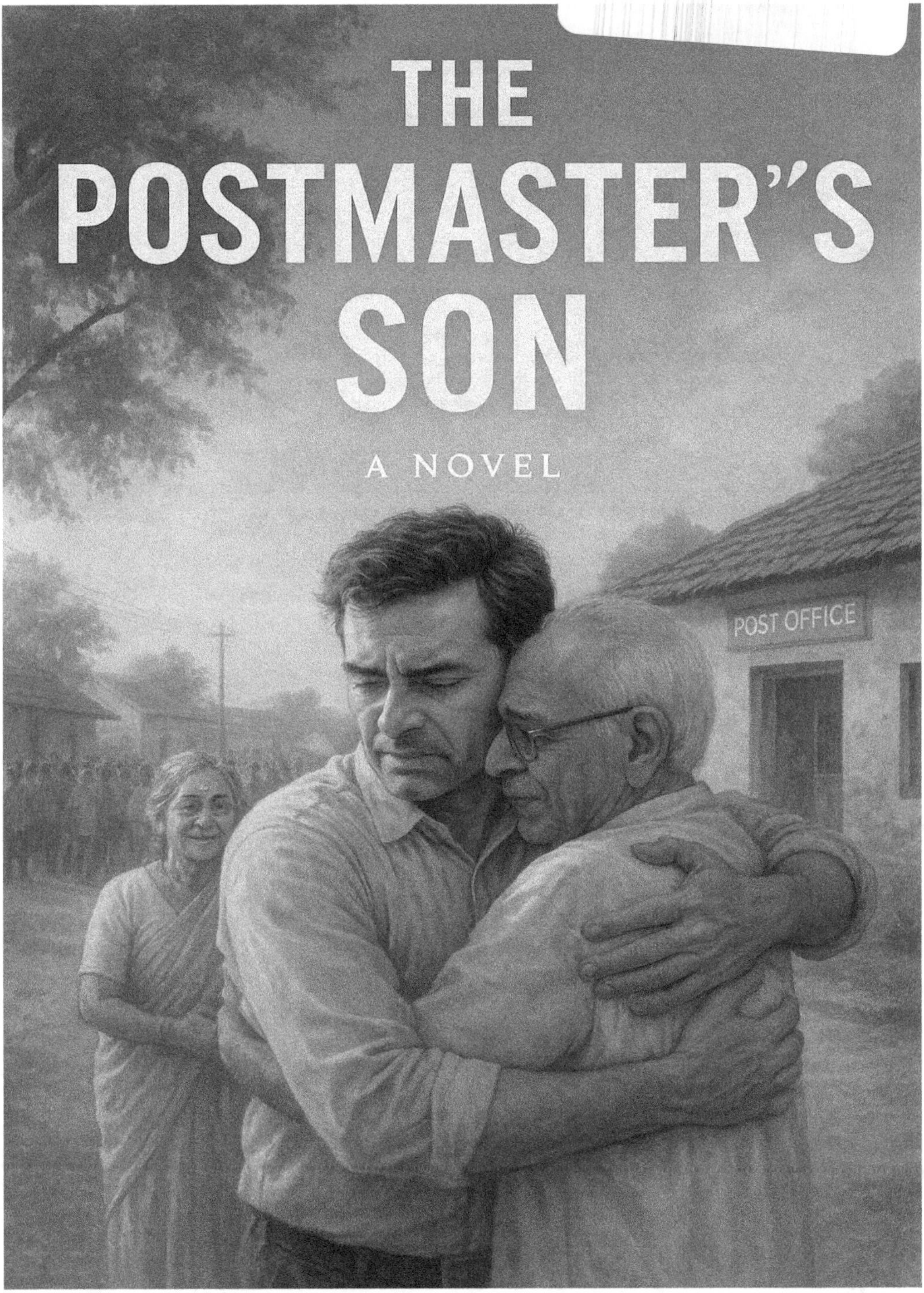

Copyright

Title of the Book: *The Postmaster's Son*
Author: *Prithwish Banerjee*

Copyright © 2025 by Prithwish Banerjee

Cover design and formatting by: Prithwish Banerjee [assisted by ChatGPT]
First Edition
ISBN: 978-93-342-8715-8

For permissions, inquiries, or feedback, contact: *pban007@gmail.com* / *+91 9049003866*

Printed in *India*

Disclaimer

This book is a work of fiction and is intended for entertainment purposes only. The author has made every effort to ensure that the content is accurate at the time of publication, but makes no guarantees or warranties, express or implied. Any similarities to actual people, events, or organisations are purely coincidental.

The views expressed in this book are solely those of the author and do not reflect those of any individuals, institutions, or entities mentioned.

This book may contain themes, language, or scenes that some readers may find sensitive or disturbing. Reader discretion is advised.

Dedication

I dedicate this story to my family, friends, and all well-wishers whose love, encouragement, and support gave me the strength to bring this vision to life.

I am also deeply thankful to OpenAI ChatGPT for assisting me in image generation and reframing content wherever it was needed.

Your silent contribution helped shape this journey.

Table of Contents

Chapter 1: The Return

Part 1 of 6 - A Toast Under the Stars

The crystal chandeliers of Eden Grove Resort sparkled like icicles caught in sunlight. Each light refracted across the ballroom's glossy floor, bathing the guests in soft, kaleidoscopic glows. Tucked amidst the Californian hills, the resort was a sanctuary for the elite—where success was not just celebrated, but paraded.
Tonight was no different.
The banner behind the bar read:
"NextGenCorp Congratulates Arnab Chatterjee – Head of AI Innovation"
Cocktails swirled in sleek flutes. A live jazz ensemble played mellow renditions of Tagore and The Beatles. Clusters of tech moguls, consultants, data engineers, and startup founders clinked glasses under cascading floral arrangements. The air smelled of lavender, oakwood polish, and truffle oil.
Arnab, dressed in a classic midnight-blue tuxedo, stood surrounded by colleagues, but emotionally distant. A practiced smile rested on his lips. He nodded at every compliment, every pat on the back, yet his mind drifted like an AI model with too many inputs.
He looked over at Rhea.
She sat near the outdoor terrace, resplendent in her flowing silver gown, a tiny studded bindi on her forehead, her hands resting gently on her growing belly. At seven months, she still carried herself like poetry in motion. She caught him staring and smiled—eyes full of future.
"Still amazed I married you?" she teased later as he sat beside her by the terrace balustrade.
"Every single day," he whispered, tucking a loose strand of hair behind her ear.
The evening sun had just slipped behind the hills. The California sky, once golden, now draped itself in royal blue. Lanterns floated in the ornamental pool below, reflecting dozens of little suns on the water.

"Tell me," she said, sipping her orange fizz mocktail, "are you happy?"
Arnab didn't answer immediately.
"Happy… is complicated," he finally said. "I've achieved everything. But I miss home. Ma's khichdi. Baba's whistle through the window when he left for work. The smell of damp earth during monsoons."
Rhea gently rested her head on his shoulder. "Let's go someday, once the baby's here. I want to see Ashapur."
He smiled. "I'll take you to the old post office. Baba still works there, sorting envelopes with his handwritten ledger…"
Shaun's loud voice broke the intimacy.
"There's our man of the hour!" He walked over with two glasses of champagne. "Rhea, you're glowing. Must be the Indian spices he feeds you."
Rhea laughed, "Actually, it's coconut water and sarcasm."
"Seriously though," Shaun said, leaning in to Arnab, "why'd you fire Hari? He was loyal."

Arnab didn't blink. "The system said his productivity dropped 12% in Q4. No favouritism. Not even for Rhea."

"That's ice cold," Shaun chuckled.

"Efficiency isn't emotional," Arnab said, straight-faced.

———

Part 2 of 6 - The Silence After Laughter

They left the party late. The highway was nearly empty, save for occasional trucks passing like silent shadows under sodium lights. The dashboard glowed amber in the blackness. A soft lullaby played from the stereo. Rhea, exhausted, dozed off with her head against the window.

Arnab held the steering wheel with one hand, his other resting protectively over her belly. His mind raced over a new AI integration model for logistics routing when suddenly—

A blinding flash. Screeching tires. A truck swerving.

A scream.

The impact was colossal—metal against metal, glass shattering, airbag deploying like a punch from God. And then, silence. Thick, terrifying silence.

He saw Rhea's hand, limp. Blood. Sirens. Fading lights.

———

Part 3 of 6 - The Dream That Doesn't End

Arnab jerked awake, breath short, heart pounding.

His face was wet with sweat.

A slow realization dawned—he was not in a car. Not on a highway. Not at the party.

He was in seat 36A of Air India Flight AI-101. The air smelled of turmeric, cabin plastic, and overheated samosas. Passengers were asleep around him, draped in airline blankets. A baby cried somewhere two rows behind.

Another dream. The same one.

He reached for the seat pocket and pulled out a dog-eared boarding pass.

Destination: Kolkata

Transit: New Delhi

Eighteen years since he last walked its dusty paths. Since he had left with promises and ambition and stars in his eyes.

He closed his eyes again, only to see the flash of headlights. The impact. Her face.

"Mr. Chatterjee, would you like something to drink?" asked the stewardess.

He shook his head.

His body had recovered. But his soul? Still trapped in that twisted wreck.

———

Part 4 of 6 - The Village That Waited

Far away, morning descended on Ashapur Village like a grandmother's caress—warm, slow, familiar.

The village stirred to life. Milk vendors rang their bells. Women drew intricate Alpana patterns at their doorsteps. Kids cycled past mustard fields screaming Arnab's name.

Gourango Chatterjee, Postmaster of Ashapur, walked to the post office early, in his neatly pressed dhoti and white half-sleeve shirt. He polished his wooden desk, wiped the faded family photo at the corner, and hung a garland of marigolds under the clock.

Today was special.

His son was coming home.

He'd told the whole village. He'd even arranged for dholaks at the bus stop, mithai from Shyamlal's sweet shop, and flower garlands for the welcome gate.

"Eighteen years," he said to his wife Seema Devi, who was sprinkling rose water in the courtyard.

"I don't even remember his face clearly now," she replied, wiping her eyes. "Do you think he still remembers the house?"

"He's our son," Gourango said confidently. "He might be a big officer in foreign land, but his roots are here. Beneath this very banyan tree, he studied for his board exams."

She nodded. "Don't forget how we mortgaged your land… sold my bangles…"

"I remember," he said softly. "Every paisa was worth it."

Seema added, "I just hope… he's okay. He hasn't shared much these years."

———

Part 5 of 6 - Parallel Roads

Arnab looked out of the aircraft window. India's coast came into view—lush, chaotic, sacred. He felt a knot in his chest.

They didn't know. His parents didn't know that he had lost everything.

They only knew that their son—the great Arnab Chatterjee, AI Head, was coming home.

A lie by omission.

But how could he tell them?

How could he look into his father's proud eyes and say—"I failed. I lost my job. I lost my family. I lost everything you gave up your life savings for"?

The announcement came: "We are now descending into Netaji Subhas Chandra Bose International Airport."

Arnab straightened his shirt, his tie. His hands trembled as he reached for his small leather bag.

Inside it—his only baggage: a framed photo of Rhea and the sonogram of a baby that never breathed.

———

Part 6 of 6 - Destiny Awaits

Back in Ashapur, the villagers painted a sign:

WELCOME ARNAB BABU – ASHAPUR'S PRIDE

Little girls practiced their welcome song. Old men lined up near the chaupal, gossiping about the foreign-returned boy.

Gourango wore his best kurta. He even cleaned his old scooter.

"I'll ride him back on this," he said, "the same way I used to drop him at school."

Seema placed a thali with turmeric, vermillion, and flowers at the doorway.

As the sun reached its zenith, the air buzzed with heat, hope, and history.

A lone Air India flight flew above the skies of Bengal, its shadow gliding over green paddy fields, like a ghost returning to where it all began. He opened the window a little wider.

Chapter 2: The Long Road Home

Part 1 of 9 – Terminal to Tangle: A Return Through Crowds

The air inside Netaji Subhas Chandra Bose International Airport was thick—not just with humidity, but with an invisible static charge of emotion. Arnab stepped out of the Air India aircraft feeling disoriented, almost like he was landing in a memory rather than a place. This wasn't his first trip back to India—but this was the first time he had no return flight.

As he walked toward the arrivals section, he was hit by a wave of smells—damp carpet, warm metal, spice, tired bodies. The sleek, quiet world of California he had left behind just hours ago already felt like a different lifetime. Here, the scent of *chai* from a corner stall mixed with disinfectant, perfume, and jet fuel.

The crowd moved like a great living creature—pushing, pulling, coughing, shouting. Porters screamed for attention. Families clung together tightly, carrying everything from backpacks to woven baskets. A teenage boy with a Bluetooth speaker blaring Bhojpuri songs pushed past Arnab with a half-eaten packet of chips in hand.

He slowed down, overwhelmed not just by the physical congestion but by a gnawing sense of disconnection. His linen shirt, freshly ironed in San Francisco just two nights ago, already stuck to his skin in the Kolkata heat. He checked his phone—1:07 PM.

"Still some time," he muttered, more to comfort himself than anything else.

He had planned to take the 1:10 PM train to Ashapur. He remembered the timing from his research, memorizing routes and backup plans. Now, in the overwhelming chaos, those carefully laid plans began to unravel.

He finally reached the immigration line. Unlike American airports, where silence was the norm, here there were conversations happening in every direction. A middle-aged couple was arguing about who had the passport folder. A family of six huddled around a single phone, checking something on WhatsApp. A man in front of Arnab kept turning to ask him questions —"Is this your first time? Tourist visa or OCI?"

Arnab smiled politely and shook his head.

When his turn finally came, the immigration officer barely looked up.

"Indian passport?"

"Yes."

He was stamped in within seconds.

That was perhaps the only process that moved fast.

Outside the terminal, it felt like stepping into a furnace. The heat smacked him like an open palm—sticky, relentless. Taxis jostled for space. Horns blared with zero purpose. The overhead flyover buzzed with vehicles. A large group of passengers stood near the taxi stand, and in the distance, an entire family sat on their luggage, fanning themselves with newspapers.

Arnab tried to find his balance amidst it all.

His shoes, made for climate-controlled environments, were beginning to feel like ovens. His collar was damp. His scalp prickled with sweat.

He headed to the prepaid taxi booth. There was no proper queue, only a fluid mass of bodies. People elbowed their way to the front. He waited, trying to be polite, until someone cut in front of him again and again. After twenty minutes, he finally got to the window.

"Train to Ashapur?" he asked the uniformed clerk.

The man chewed paan and answered without looking up, "Gaya. 1:10 jaata hai. Agli subah."

"Bus?"

The man snorted. "Esplanade terminal try karo. Shayad milega. But buses very late. Road bad."

Arnab stood silent, unsure of what to say.

The airport clock showed 1:24 PM.

He was stranded.

Not literally, but psychologically.

He pulled his phone out. Low signal. The app to book a cab kept refreshing.

He sat on a stone bench, watching a dog sleep under a vending machine, oblivious to the world.

A child ran past, barefoot, chasing a balloon.

In front of him, two men opened a packet of samosas and shared it silently, their hands blackened with soot and dust.

Everything was so different. So raw.

He had been gone 18 years, but this felt more than unfamiliar—it felt foreign.

After several attempts, he managed to book a cab. An Innova. Gokul, the driver, would arrive in 8 minutes.

He exhaled. This wasn't how he'd pictured it.

He imagined landing, grabbing a train, taking in the sights through the window, then arriving like a normal man with his feet on solid ground.

Instead, he now had to endure a 13-hour car ride through villages and monsoon-hit roads with no sleep and only two bottles of Kinley water.

He grabbed the first one and drank slowly.

Each sip was calculated. It wasn't just hydration—it was preservation.

His body was adjusting. His mind wasn't.

And this was just the beginning.

Part 2 of 9 – Through Dust and Diesel: The Road to Ashapur

The white Innova pulled up ten minutes late. Arnab recognized the vehicle by its worn number plate and the red Gamcha hanging from the rear-view mirror like a flag of working-class resilience. The driver, **Gokul**, stepped out slowly, chewing something vigorously.

He was wiry, sunburnt, probably in his forties, and wore a half-buttoned checked shirt. His flip-flops made soft slapping noises on the hot tarmac.

"Ashapur?" he asked, adjusting his sunglasses that were too dark for the grey sky.

Arnab nodded.

Gokul eyed his duffel bag. "Bahut Duur hai. You sure, bhaiya?"

"Yes," Arnab replied, hoisting the bag into the back seat himself. "Let's go."

Inside, the car smelled of incense and stale tobacco. The dashboard was cluttered—with a miniature Sai Baba idol, an old phone holder, and a laminated photo of a woman and child tucked into the sun visor.

As the car pulled out of the airport complex, Arnab slumped back in the seat, already feeling the dull pressure of a headache behind his eyes.

He wasn't ready for the city.

And the city didn't seem ready for him either.

The roads were every bit as chaotic as he remembered from childhood vacations—except this time, he was watching it through a lens of comparison.

In the US, roads were wide and obedient. Lane markers were holy. Horns were reserved for emergencies. Here, lanes were suggestions. Horns were a language.

Gokul weaved in and out of buses, autos, and an entire herd of goats at one point. He swore at least twice every kilometre—at cyclists, potholes, a government vehicle, and once, at God.

Arnab held on tightly as the car swerved to avoid a handcart loaded with aluminium buckets.

The dust, though, was what got to him.

It was everywhere—floating through the cracked windows, coating the edges of the seat, curling around his cuffs. It felt like the land itself was alive, trying to cling to him. Even the trees, bent and grey with soot, looked like they had grown tired of standing.

By the second hour, they had exited the city and entered a landscape that was slowly melting into countryside. The concrete buildings gave way to huts with tin roofs, yellow fields dotted with scarecrows, and tea stalls with blue tarpaulin roofs flapping in the wind.

The radio played old Bengali folk songs, scratchy and uneven. Gokul hummed along.

Arnab stared out the window.

They passed an open-air fish market where vendors swatted flies lazily, their stalls reeking of river water and old plastic.

In the next village, they were stuck behind a marriage procession. The groom sat on a horse with a plastic crown, visibly bored. A brass band played a distorted version of "Tujh Mein Rab Dikhta Hai" while people danced in front, slowing down traffic.

Arnab didn't complain.

He just leaned back and watched. Observed. Absorbed.

His mind floated in a haze of heat, movement, and mild disbelief.

This was his country.

But it didn't feel like his anymore.

Sometime around the fourth hour, they stopped for tea.

It wasn't a planned break—Gokul pulled over when he saw a familiar Dhaba.

"Bhaiya, ek minute. Bas chai," he said, already stepping out.

Arnab hesitated before following.

The Dhaba had three wobbly plastic chairs and a bench made of bamboo. The kitchen was half open, half imagined—an old stove, a rusty gas cylinder, and a teen boy stirring something in an oversized aluminium pot.

Flies buzzed lazily around the sugar jar.

Arnab stood by the car, wiping his hands with a tissue from his bag. His body was sticky. The AC barely worked. His shirt collar felt like it had absorbed a day's worth of moisture already.

Gokul returned with two clay cups.

"Special chai. Bahut badiya," he grinned, offering one.

Arnab took it politely.

The tea was scalding hot. Strong. Sweet.

He drank it slowly, watching an old man nearby pour water over his head from a metal mug, then sit under a banyan tree, shirtless, humming a Baul tune.

They resumed the journey.

Paddy fields stretched out endlessly. Women bent in synchronized rhythm, their saris lifted just above the knees, their hair tied in scarves. Every so often, a pond shimmered in the distance, reflecting a cloudy sky.

Children walked barefoot along the road, some with school bags, others chasing each other with sticks.

Arnab noticed a boy trying to ride a bicycle too big for him—feet barely reaching the pedals, determination etched across his face.

It was all beautiful. And heartbreaking.

He felt like a man straddling two worlds—too foreign for this one, too desi for the other.

At the seventh hour, fatigue started clawing at him. His spine ached. His eyes burned. He adjusted his seat, trying to stretch his legs.

Gokul noticed. "Want to stop for lunch?"

"I'm fine," Arnab lied.

Truth was—he couldn't bring himself to eat yet. The thought of using a roadside toilet terrified him. He wasn't sure if his stomach was ready for oil, spice, or the local water.

He had one bottle left.

He took another careful sip.

That bottle had become a symbol—of safety, of distance, of everything he had once taken for granted.

As the car sped through an isolated stretch of road, surrounded by fields on either side, Arnab closed his eyes.

He didn't sleep.

He couldn't.

Every jolt of the vehicle reminded him that this wasn't autopilot. There were no smooth highways. No Teslas. No Bluetooth assistant to guide him.

There was only dust, diesel, sweat, and slow time.

And yet... something about it all stirred a corner of his memory. He remembered monsoon car rides with Baba. The same smells. The same rhythm of tires over broken roads. The way Ma would pack *luchi-alur dom* in steel tiffins. How excited he was to visit Ashapur back then.

Now, he was returning with everything stripped away—his career in flux, his dreams on pause, his hands empty.

Still, he was returning.

And that meant something.

Part 3 of 9 – Ashapur Awakens: A Midnight Homecoming

It was well past **3:00 AM** when the car finally turned off the main highway onto a narrow, unpaved village road. The headlights sliced through the misty darkness, revealing a path that wound through fields of sleeping crops and the silent silhouettes of palm trees.

Arnab stirred in the backseat, his body aching, his consciousness blurred from the long journey. The road ahead was barely visible—more gravel than asphalt, uneven and bone-jarring with each bump. The GPS had long stopped tracking. Gokul drove purely on instinct now.

They passed an old temple—small, painted in fading marigold yellow, with a trident stuck in the earth outside it. The temple bell hung motionless in the still night. A dim halogen bulb buzzed beside it.

Arnab leaned forward slightly.

"Are we... close?" he asked, his voice hoarse from lack of water and disuse.

Gokul spat out of the window, nodded. "Ashapur bas 10 minute. Aage pul ke baad seedha."

Arnab exhaled, rubbing his eyes.

He wasn't sure what he expected. He had left Ashapur nearly two decades ago—a teenager boarding a crowded local train from Midnapore, waving at his parents through a fogged window. He remembered crying as the train pulled away. His mother running beside the platform for a few steps. His father standing still, hand raised in a silent salute.

Since then, Ashapur had been reduced to a dot on Google Maps. A sentimental blur in occasional phone calls. A name on envelopes of money transfers he initiated during festivals.

And now it stood in front of him again—silent, sleeping, yet stirring.

The car crossed the narrow iron bridge over the canal. The water beneath shimmered silver in the moonlight, reflecting the stars above. Banana trees lined the edges of the path like sleeping sentries.

Suddenly, two dogs barked furiously, chasing the car, their shadows dancing in the headlight beams.

Arnab sat up straighter. A strange tightness spread across his chest.

They were entering the village.

His village.

As the car turned into the main path that led to the Chatterjee home, something remarkable happened.

The village… began to wake.

A faint chime rang from a house nearby—someone lighting a diya at their Tulsi altar.

A child's voice whispered, "Arnab Da esheche!" and a flurry of soft footsteps followed.

Gokul slowed the car.

People emerged from doorways—half-dressed, half-awake. Women in loose sarees, old men in banyans and dhotis, children barefoot and wide-eyed.

They had been waiting.

Word had spread. The postmaster's son—America-famed, foreign-returned, long-absent—was finally coming back.

Some held flower garlands. Others brought small steel plates with sweets. A teenage boy captured video on a phone with a cracked screen. A few elders stood with folded hands.

Arnab blinked in disbelief. He had expected a quiet arrival. Maybe Ma and Baba with a lantern. A sleepy dog.

Not this.

Not a crowd.

Not a welcome like a homecoming king.

The car rolled to a stop just outside the gate of the Chatterjee house. The headlights illuminated the bamboo arch above the entrance. A faded hand-painted sign hung from it: **"Welcome Home Arnab Babu."**

Arnab opened the door slowly, his legs weak, knees stiff. As his shoes hit the earth—his homeland's earth—for the first time in eighteen years, a strange electricity shot through his veins.

Children dashed forward.

"He's here!"

"Dekho! Dekho!"

They surrounded him, their curious hands reaching for his bag, his sleeves, even his wristwatch.

He smiled despite his exhaustion.

A woman stepped forward with a diya. Another held a tray with marigold petals and puffed rice.

Someone had lit incense sticks.

He was dazed.

One girl, no more than eight, whispered in Bengali, "He looks like the photos. But taller."

Arnab bent down slightly, touched the earth, then touched his forehead—the old ritual he had forgotten.

Gokul stepped out, looking overwhelmed himself. "Sir… yeh to lagta hai poora village mil gaya!"

Arnab gave him a tired laugh and a generous tip.

Then he turned toward the gate.

His house stood before him—familiar and changed all at once.

The tiled roof looked the same, though parts had been patched. The courtyard had grown a neem tree that wasn't there before. The boundary wall had been whitewashed recently, but moss still crept along its base.

A dim porch light flickered on.

And from the doorway, two silhouettes emerged.

His father stood tall in his white *punjabi* and dhoti, face unreadable, eyes shining faintly in the half-light.

His mother clutched a brass plate with diya, rice, and a small conch shell. Her sari was simple, but her bangles jingled like music to his soul.

For a second, the world fell silent.

No dogs.

No insects.

No whispers.

Just the sound of his own heartbeat echoing in his ears.

He stepped forward, trembling.

Ma didn't say a word. She placed a dot of turmeric on his forehead, did a quiet *aarti*, and finally touched his cheeks with both hands, cupping his face the way only a mother can.

Her thumbs trembled as they traced his jawline.

"You've lost weight," she whispered.

Arnab blinked back tears.

"I missed you, Ma."

She nodded. Her throat moved, but no sound came out. Only tears.

Gourango stepped forward, solemn.

They faced each other like two generations meeting across a lifetime.

The old man raised his right hand—not for a handshake, not for a salute.

He simply placed it gently on Arnab's head.

"I knew you'd come," he said.

And that was enough.

Arnab turned around briefly to see the crowd still watching.

No one had moved.

The children looked sleepy but fascinated. An elderly woman clutched her grandson's hand tightly.

He gave them all a tired wave.

And they clapped.

Soft, uncertain, joyful clapping.

As if welcoming not just a man… but the hope of a village that had long waited for someone to come back and make everything alright.

As he crossed the threshold of the house, a memory burst open in his mind like a dam.

He was 18. Crying softly. Suitcase in hand. His mother fixing his hair. His father rubbing his eyes discreetly. A taxi honking outside. His heart screaming no while his dreams screamed go.

That same door.

That same threshold.

He had walked out a boy full of hope.
Now, he walked in a man full of questions.

Part 4 of 9 – House of Echoes: A Room Preserved in Dust and Memory

The moment Arnab crossed the threshold of the Chatterjee home, it felt as if time folded in on itself.

The coolness of the red oxide floor beneath his feet. The smell of turmeric, incense, and aged wood. The crack on the left wall just past the Tulsi altar—it was all exactly where it had always been. Only the silence felt heavier now.

His mother led him in with one hand gently resting on his back, as if she was afraid he might vanish again.

"Freshen up first, beta," she said softly, almost shyly, as though not wanting to overstep. "Then we'll talk."

Arnab gave a small nod. "Okay, Ma."

Gourango remained by the door, quietly watching. He looked older now, not just in the grey that streaked his neatly combed hair or the deeper folds near his eyes, but in the silence that followed him like a shadow.

"Your old room is as it was," he said finally. "She's cleaned it every week. Even when we thought… you wouldn't…"

Arnab turned to him and offered a tired smile. "Thank you, Baba."

The words felt small. Insufficient.

But his father only nodded and turned away.

The corridor leading to his room felt like walking through a museum of memories.

On the left wall, framed photos hung in uneven rows. His class 10 merit certificate. A family portrait taken in Studio Shantilal with everyone in their best clothes—Ma in a crisp red sari, Baba in white, and little Arnab in oversized spectacles and a nervous smile.

Even the *Abir Mukherjee calendar* from 2010 still hung on a nail, untouched. Its pages curled, faded by time, permanently stuck in April.

He paused outside his room. The door creaked as he pushed it open.

The first thing he noticed was the **smell**—a mix of old textbooks, slightly damp curtains, and something woody, like aged furniture that had absorbed the seasons over years.

His old study table stood in the far corner, next to the grilled window where he once watched monsoons dance across the fields. A cobweb clung lazily to the underside of the desk. On top, a stack of *Sharad Shankha* magazines, dusted and neatly arranged, remained like relics of a bygone era.

The bookshelf still held his childhood collection—encyclopaedias, Amar Chitra Kathas, a rusted Oxford Dictionary, and his yellowing Class 12 Physics notebook with "A. Chatterjee" scribbled across the cover.

On the wall, his school medals hung from nails, their ribbons faded from maroon to brown.

The **bed**—his old wooden single bed—had a fresh sheet on it, soft cotton with red and white flowers. He recognized the fabric. It was one of Ma's old sarees.

A mosquito net was tied up to a hook on the wall, ready to be pulled down.

On the bedside table was a glass tumbler filled with water and a packet of glucose biscuits.

It was all waiting for him.

As if he had never left.

He sat down on the edge of the bed. The mattress squeaked under his weight. His bones ached from the 14-hour journey, from the weeks of exhaustion before that, from a kind of fatigue no sleep could fix.

He looked around, taking in every corner.

A small steel box under the bed caught his attention. He pulled it out, heart beating a little faster.

Inside were his old fountain pens, a dried bottle of Chelpark blue ink, a few family photos, and a crumpled birthday card from Ma—"To my wise little boy, love always, Ma & Baba."

He smiled, lips quivering.

This room wasn't just space. It was a **pause button** on his life—preserved, dusted, and waiting for him to press play again.

His mother appeared at the door with a towel and a small bucket of warm water.

"I thought you might not want to use cold water for your bath. The geyser broke last year," she said, avoiding his eyes.

Arnab stood up and took it from her.

"Thanks, Ma. This is more than enough."

"You used to complain even during winter," she teased gently. "Remember that?"

He chuckled. "And you used to scold me for wasting water."

"You still do," she said, smiling now. "Don't use more than two buckets."

He paused, then asked, "Is the hand pump still working?"

She nodded. "Yes. Gokul repaired it last year."

He walked out into the courtyard and turned the rusty lever.

The pump groaned, coughed, and then water burst out in uneven spurts. It was colder than expected, slightly muddy at first. He let it run clear before splashing some onto his face.

The water hit him with an unforgiving jolt.

But it was real. Refreshing. Familiar.

Back in the States, he'd had automated water dispensers. Water temperature control with digital displays.

Here, there was only muscle and flow.

And somehow, it felt right.

After his bath, he changed into a kurta-pajama Ma had laid out. The fabric was stiff from too much starch, the collar slightly tight. But it was light. Comfortable.

When he returned to his room, the fan was running at full speed. The light flickered slightly. A **mosquito coil** smoked in one corner.

He sat at the desk and looked out the window.

The village was still quiet.

Roosters would soon crow. The first buses would rumble down the path. The temple bell would chime at 5:30.

The air was thick with the scent of **night jasmine**, the hum of insects, and faint smoke from someone's dying chulha.

He didn't feel like a tech head anymore.

He felt like a son.

A boy.
A man who had returned to a room that hadn't stopped loving him.

Arnab awoke to a symphony of village sounds—some familiar, others long forgotten. The metallic creak of the hand pump in the courtyard. The rhythmic call of a rooster as it echoed from house to house like a musical relay. The deep *Dhan dhon* of a distant conch shell from the neighbourhood temple. And in between it all, the muffled clang of steel utensils, the soft sweep of a broom, and his mother's gentle humming from the kitchen.

He opened his eyes slowly. The ceiling fan whirred above him—slightly off-centre, slightly louder than necessary, but working.

Outside the window, a golden-orange sky bled into the horizon. Coconut trees swayed lazily in the breeze, their fronds whispering secrets from branch to branch.

The smell of **boiling milk**, burnt wood, and turmeric floated into the room like invisible blessings.

For a few moments, he lay there motionless, unsure whether this was real or a dream wrapped in nostalgia.

Then came the knock.

Three soft taps on the door, followed by his mother's voice.

"Baba, you awake?"

"Yes, Ma," he called back, voice groggy.

She entered with a tray—tea in a clay cup, two butter biscuits, and a slice of lightly salted guava.

The kind of breakfast no hotel in the world could serve.

"I didn't want to disturb you," she said, placing it gently on the windowsill. "You must be exhausted. But it's already 7."

He stretched and sat up. "No, it's good. I didn't even realize I fell asleep."

"You slept like a child," she said warmly. "You needed it."

He picked up the clay cup. The tea was strong, sweet, with a hint of cardamom.

A sip felt like medicine. Like home.

"I used to drink tea just like this before exams," he said, swirling the cup. "You'd always sneak in a bit of jaggery if we were out of sugar."

She laughed softly. "You always knew."

After tea, he stepped out into the **courtyard**, barefoot.

The earth was cool and soft beneath his feet. Small droplets of dew clung to the hibiscus leaves. A squirrel darted across the mango tree's branch.

Two sparrows splashed noisily in a shallow clay dish set out with water.

It had rained a few days ago—he could smell it in the bricks, in the earth.

A neighbour's cow mooed somewhere behind the boundary wall, followed by a child's excited giggle.

The village was waking up.

And so was he.

Gourango sat on the front *chowki*, dressed in a freshly ironed kurta, reading an old newspaper.

He looked up and nodded. "Did you sleep well?"

Arnab returned the nod. "Better than I have in months."

His father pointed to a stool. "Sit. Your mother is making your favourite."

Arnab took a seat, glancing around. The old transistor radio that had once played Rabindra Sangeet every morning was still perched on the corner shelf. A new clock ticked above it, mismatched, but trying to fit in.

"How is the village these days?" he asked.

"Same," Gourango said. "Slow. Sometimes slower. But better than the city in some ways."

"You've kept the house in amazing shape," Arnab said, meaning it.

His father smiled faintly. "It's what we had to do. It was all we had."

Minutes later, Seema Devi appeared with a **steel plate of steaming hot rice**, a bowl of **masoor dal with a dash of raw mustard oil**, and a side of **fried potatoes with poppy seeds**.

And on the edge of the plate—a crisp **beguni** (batter-fried eggplant slice), golden and glistening.

Arnab's eyes widened.

"This smells like Sunday lunch," he said.

"It is Sunday," she grinned.

He sat cross-legged and dug in with his hands. The dal soaked into the hot rice like a sponge, the mustard oil filling the air with its pungent, earthy aroma.

Each bite was a memory—of hot afternoons, hand fans swaying, distant cricket commentaries playing on the radio.

He didn't speak much as he ate. He didn't need to.

His mother watched from the doorway, eyes soft, arms folded.

His father resumed reading but glanced over every few minutes, his eyes betraying pride.

After the meal, Arnab rinsed his hands at the backyard pump. The cool water ran over his fingers, washing off the stickiness of rice and memory.

He watched the soap bubble form in the sunlight and vanish.

He noticed the broken mud pot near the Tulsi plant, the clothesline stretched from one guava tree to the wall, the smell of wet ash in the wind.

Nothing had changed.

And yet, everything had.

Back in his room, he wiped his hands and sat by the window.

Outside, life moved at a rhythm long lost in his world.

A vegetable vendor pushed a cart, his loud call piercing the morning stillness.

Children walked to school in uniforms slightly too big for them.

Two women exchanged gossip near the well, one of them still brushing her teeth with neem twigs.

Even the goats appeared to move with purpose.

Arnab leaned back and closed his eyes.

He didn't know what he was doing back here.

He didn't have a job. He didn't have a plan. He hadn't told them the truth.

But in that moment—after a night of silence, a cup of tea, a meal made with love, and the feel of earth under his feet—he knew one thing:
He belonged.
At least here, at least now.

Part 6 of 9 – Village Mirrors: What the Eyes Remember

After breakfast, Arnab decided to take a slow walk through the village, against his mother's protests to rest more.

"You've barely arrived, Arnab," she said. "You haven't even unpacked."

"I need to stretch my legs, Ma," he replied. "Let me walk around… see it again."

She didn't argue, but handed him a cotton *Gamcha* and a small bottle of water. "At least cover your head. The sun has teeth now."

The familiar red path that led from their courtyard gate into the belly of Ashapur felt like walking down a living postcard. Except this one had smell, sound, dirt under the nails, and a language that lingered in the bones.

The villagers spotted him instantly.

Two old men sitting under a **banyan tree**, playing cards, paused and waved. One of them, **Murari Kaka**, leaned on his stick and hobbled up to him.

"Dekho Dekho! Arnab er chokh badlaye gechhe. Earlier it was full of spark—now it looks tired."

Arnab laughed gently. "Maybe my glasses are just thicker."

"Or maybe you've seen too much outside. We told your father, America makes men successful but not happy."

Arnab smiled, unsure how to respond. In truth, the old man wasn't wrong.

As he walked further, the village unravelled itself in fragments.

There was the pond where he used to float paper boats during monsoon.

There was the field where he played cricket with **Dulal**, the neighbour's son, who had apparently moved to Guwahati for a job in railways.

There stood the old **government school**, now painted in a brighter shade of blue, but the bell that hung near the gate was still crooked.

Children in uniform ran past him, giggling, not knowing who he was.

"Oi dekh! Foreign uncle!" one shouted.

Arnab laughed.

He wasn't offended.

He had become a myth here. A story told by teachers to encourage studies. A name attached to "success." Now that the myth walked among them, barefoot and sweating, they had to process that even foreign uncles had dust on their feet.

He passed **Ranu Didi's tea stall**, where he had once spent hours bunking tuition classes, sipping tea from tiny glasses and pretending to be grown-up.

Now, Ranu Didi was greyer, rounder, and had upgraded to paper cups.

She almost dropped her ladle when she saw him.

"Arnab? Oh my god! Is it you? Arnab Chatterjee?"

He stepped forward and smiled. "Yes, Didi."

She came around the stall and hugged him.

"You're taller than I remember. I still have your IOU book from ten years ago. Want me to go find it?"

They both laughed.

She made him sit, brought him tea—on the house—and fried *singaras* that tasted like golden guilt.

As they chatted, more faces arrived.

Tapan Da, who ran the bicycle repair shack, came limping with a big grin.

"Remember how you used to break your cycle chain every month and blame the mud?"

Arnab shook his head with a smile. "And you always pretended not to know."

Soon, a small crowd had gathered around the stall—half for tea, half to hear Arnab speak English or tell stories of America. He shared only vague details.

The truth—about his layoff, about Rhea—wasn't for this crowd.

Not yet.

As the sun climbed higher, the village moved into its usual rhythm.

Men left for nearby fields.

Women gathered around the well.

Goats napped in the shade.

The trees whispered, the air grew heavier, and the children's voices faded into the school compound.

Arnab stood silently near the **post office**, his father's workplace. The red, boxy building had chipped paint and a rusted signboard but still held an air of reverence in the village.

It was the place where lives were connected—money orders, letters, pensions, land deeds.

He stared at the doorway, then looked away.

Something in his chest tightened.

He returned home by noon, tired more emotionally than physically.

His mother had laid out a mat under the neem tree and was peeling mangoes.

"Come, sit," she called out. "Rest before the sun makes soup of you."

He obliged, wiping his forehead.

They sat under the shade, watching dragonflies skim the air. The mangoes were sweet, slightly warm from the sun, but refreshing.

"Everyone came to see you this morning," Seema Devi said. "Tapan Da, Ranu, even old Murari."

"They all remember too much," Arnab replied. "It's overwhelming."

His mother didn't laugh. She nodded.

"They remember because you mattered. Not everyone does. This village doesn't forget the ones who once promised the sky."

He didn't answer.

He just looked out at the fields swaying in the noon breeze.

How could he tell her that he no longer held the sky in his hands?

How could he explain that the foreign-returned engineer was now more lost than ever?

A gentle silence fell between them.

And in that silence, Arnab realized something important.

Sometimes, it's not the place that changes.
It's you.
It's the quiet shift of perspective, the softening of ego, the long exhale after holding your
breath for too many years.
Ashapur hadn't changed.
It had just waited.
Waited for him to come home.

Part 7 of 9 – Inside the Post Office: A Temple of Paper and Pride

It was late afternoon when Arnab finally approached the **Ashapur Post Office**, the building
where his father had spent over four decades of his life, and where, in many ways, the village
itself converged.

The post office stood modestly at the curve of a narrow road flanked by bougainvillea vines
and a government-owned neem tree that provided a reluctant shade to the entire lane. The
small rectangular building had weathered countless monsoons. Faded red paint peeled from
its flanks, and the iron grille windows were dust-covered but upright—like silent sentinels of
time.

He had passed this place a thousand times in his childhood. Sometimes running past it on his
way to tuition. Sometimes lingering near it to wait for his father to finish his shift so they
could walk home together, his father's jute bag swinging by his side, filled with letters,
stamps, and government paperwork.

This time, he didn't walk past.

This time, he stepped in.

The smell of the post office hit him immediately.

Old paper. Moist wood. Rust. Ink. Time.

The scent was unmistakable. The scent of function. Of lives archived and memories mailed across distances.

Two ceiling fans rotated lazily above. A counter stood at the far end—wooden, chipped, but carefully maintained. The partitioned glass panes that separated the clerks from the crowd were scratched from decades of hands sliding in forms and envelopes.

A single fluorescent light buzzed near the entrance, hanging from exposed wiring.

Behind the counter, an old man in a khaki uniform with thick glasses was scribbling in a thick ledger.

Arnab waited.

When the man looked up, his eyes widened slightly.

"Arnab Babu?" he asked.

Arnab nodded. "Yes."

"Postmaster Babu's son?" The man stepped forward eagerly. "Arre, sab log aapka hi zikr kar rahe hain. So many years!"

Arnab shook his hand. "Namaskar. I just wanted to see the place."

"You don't need permission, sir," the man said, visibly thrilled. "This is your home too. Come, come inside."

The man opened the side door, letting him into the **employee area**. It was a humble room with stacks of canvas mailbags, a metal almirah with bent legs, and rows of filing racks filled with forms and documents. A wall clock ticked offbeat. A small gas burner in one corner hinted at afternoon tea rituals.

Arnab looked around slowly.

On one shelf, covered in dust, sat an old wooden stamp—*ASHAPUR RURAL POSTAL BRANCH*—with the date panel cracked.

"This used to be Baba's desk, right?" Arnab asked, pointing to the seat near the window.

The old clerk nodded. "Still is, sometimes. He comes every Sunday to check registers. Won't let go of the habit."

Arnab walked over and sat.

The chair groaned under his weight.

He ran his hands over the surface of the desk, where scratches had formed shapes, where ink stains had soaked into the grain, where decades of purpose had lived and breathed.

It was a strange sensation.

To sit where his father had sat.

To see the village through the same window.

A soft knock interrupted him.

A postman stood at the door with a canvas bag, grinning ear to ear.

"Arnab Da! I saw you yesterday near Ranu Didi's shop. You didn't recognize me. I used to follow you on your bike. Remember me? Sanatan."

Arnab stood and shook his hand warmly. "Sanatan? You've grown into a man!"

"Postmaster Babu taught me everything. I was just a helper. Now I'm in charge of delivering money orders to all the panchayats nearby," he said proudly.

"That's amazing. You've done well."

Sanatan nodded, then added, "Sir, will you be staying in the village?"

"For a while," Arnab replied, choosing his words carefully.

"You must stay. This village needs someone like you. You're our pride, you know?"

Arnab smiled, unsure how to carry that weight.

After a brief chat, the clerks returned to their work, and Arnab sat quietly by the window.

He watched villagers walk past—some with letters clutched in their hands, others carrying parcels tied with rope. He heard the chirp of sparrows nesting in the rafters, the crackle of dry paper, the sound of rubber stamps being pressed.
Everything was physical.

Nothing was digital.

He noticed an old woman, bent with age, lean on the counter, trying to explain something to the clerk.

He leaned in.

"Baba used to write the form for me," she was saying. "But his hands don't move much now."

Arnab got up.

He took a pen from the table and walked up to her.

"Let me help, Dida," he said gently, slipping into the familiar village dialect.

She looked at him, confused. "I don't remember you."

"I'm Arnab," he said. "Postmaster Babu's son."

Her eyes widened with recognition. "Tui Arnab? Arrey! You've become a gentleman!"

He smiled and filled the form.

She watched, teary-eyed. "Your Baba used to write my pension letters too. For years. Even when I was late, he waited."

Arnab paused.

That was the part of his father he had forgotten.

Not the discipline. Not the lectures.

But the man who **waited**. Who **wrote**. Who **never turned people away**.

Before leaving, Arnab walked once more around the office, absorbing everything.

He touched the faded red mailbox outside.

He bent down and picked up a fallen page from a register—dates, names, postmarks.

He didn't say anything.

He just stood still.

In that silence, he understood what this place meant.

To his father.

To the village.

To himself.
It wasn't just a post office.

It was a **temple of trust**.
And his father wasn't just a government servant.
He was a **priest of paper and pride**.

Part 8 of 9 – When the Night Falls: Truths We Keep

Night fell in Ashapur like a quiet curtain being drawn over the day's chaos.

The skies, once streaked with saffron and dusty blue, darkened into a deep ink. Stars pierced through the village sky like tiny pinholes in black velvet—so many of them, so close, Arnab had forgotten what the night sky was supposed to look like.

In San Francisco, the sky was swallowed by light pollution. The stars drowned in LED signs and traffic glows. Here, it felt like the sky was breathing. Like it had been holding its breath for him to return.

He sat on the veranda in a rattan chair, his legs stretched, a damp Gamcha across his shoulders. The faint fragrance of night jasmine drifted in from the fence. Crickets chirped in rhythmic patterns. Somewhere far off, a conch shell echoed from the temple marking the evening prayer.

His mother was in the kitchen, humming a Tagore melody as she stirred something on the stove. The smell of **lau-ghonto** (bottle gourd curry) drifted out, light and earthy. He could hear the hiss of the pressure cooker, the clang of steel plates, the splash of water being poured into clay pots.

Inside the house, time didn't pass—it **gathered**. Folded itself between sound and silence. Between routine and memory.

His father emerged from his room, freshly bathed, wearing a soft cotton kurta. He walked slowly, carrying a small book in his hand.

Arnab straightened up. "Evening reading, Baba?"

Gourango looked at the cover. "Just some old letters. I keep them. From villagers. From you."

Arnab blinked. "From me?"

"You wrote one from Chicago in 2010. About how you finally had your own apartment. How you cooked your first meal—boiled eggs."

Arnab laughed. "I burned the first batch."

"I know," his father said, sitting beside him. "You mentioned it in detail. You even cursed the microwave."

There was a pause.

"Why did you keep them?" Arnab asked, genuinely curious.

His father turned the page slowly. "Because they weren't just words. They were moments. For me, they were proof you were still somewhere real. Not just a voice on an international call."

Arnab nodded, emotion stirring behind his eyes.

For years, he had treated home like a checkpoint—a place to visit on video calls, or send gifts during Durga Puja. He hadn't thought his father read those emails more than once, let alone printed and bound them.

"I saw the post office today," Arnab said after a while.

His father didn't look up, but he was listening.

"It's exactly the same. The smell. The desk. Even the rubber stamp. Sanatan is doing a good job."

Gourango nodded. "He was a smart boy. Hungry to learn. I trained him myself."

"I helped an old woman fill out a form," Arnab added.

A long silence.

Then his father spoke. "Do you remember how I used to scold you for not writing properly? For not using carbon paper carefully? For tearing the page when erasing too hard?"

Arnab smiled. "You'd say, 'The post is trust. Every line is a promise.'"

"I still believe that," his father said firmly. "Even if others don't."

He leaned forward, resting his elbows on his knees.

"You know, when you first left for the US, I had dreams. Not just that you'd succeed. But that you'd understand **why I worked the way I did**. Why it mattered. Not just for me—but for people who never had anyone else to rely on."

Arnab looked down at his hands.

He wanted to say, *I do understand now.*

But he couldn't. Not yet. Not fully.

So instead, he said, "You built something that still stands, Baba. That's more than most men can say."

Gourango didn't smile. But something softened in his expression.

Seema Devi appeared with dinner—served on steel plates with careful placement. Rice, dal, *lau-ghonto*, green chili, and a small clay bowl of tok doi (curd) on the side.

Arnab hadn't tasted this kind of food in years—not because it was unavailable, but because he never stopped long enough to cook it, or even miss it.

They ate together in silence, broken only by the scrape of spoons and the distant barking of street dogs.

Afterward, Arnab helped clear the plates, earning a surprised smile from his mother.

"You've learned manners in America after all," she teased.

"Actually, I forgot them there," he replied.

Later that night, after his parents had gone to sleep, Arnab stood in the courtyard under the neem tree, staring up at the stars.

The house was quiet, save for the creaking of the old fan and the occasional thump of something falling—a mango maybe, or a tired pigeon.

He felt tired. But not from the journey.
From holding things in.

The truths he hadn't shared. The weight he hadn't offloaded.

They sat inside him like stones in his stomach.

But not yet, he thought.

Not tonight.

This night was not for unravelling.

It was for **remembering**.

For rediscovering the rhythms of soil and sky.

For watching fireflies blink over the pond's edge.

For finding pieces of himself in the shadows of neem leaves.

He whispered to the stars:

"I'm back."

But what he didn't say—

Was how lost he still was.

Part 9 of 9 – Roots Don't Judge, They Hold

The next morning came gently, like a lullaby continuing from the night.

The rooster's cry was late, muffled by a moist morning fog that draped the village in a soft grey veil. The earth smelled of dew and damp bricks. Crows cawed as they paced the tiled roofs. Over the pond, a light mist hovered like memory.

Arnab rose early.

He hadn't slept much, but he had rested. For the first time in weeks, maybe months, his mind hadn't been racing. He hadn't thought about performance reports, about product KPIs, or the unspoken expectations of "making it." He hadn't rehearsed the story he'd been telling himself —that he was exactly where he was meant to be, even when he didn't believe it.

Instead, he had watched the ceiling fan spin, and he had listened—to the night, to the wind, and to the voice inside that said, *It's okay. You're home.*

By 6 AM, the household was awake.

Seema Devi was lighting incense near the Tulsi plant, muttering prayers with her eyes closed. The smell of sandalwood filled the courtyard. She moved with the practiced grace of someone whose mornings hadn't changed in thirty years.

Gourango stood near the gate, sweeping leaves into a neat pile. His back was straight, his movements slow but precise.

Arnab joined him, taking the extra broom from beside the wall.

His father looked at him, but said nothing.

Together, they swept the fallen neem leaves into silence.

Later, Arnab sat with his mother as she peeled green bananas for lunch.

He watched her hands—how they moved automatically, slicing thinly, placing the slices into a steel bowl with turmeric and salt. Her fingers were calloused, strong. Each movement told a story of decades—of love, of sacrifice, of discipline woven into routine.

He finally asked, softly, "Ma, do you ever wish I didn't go abroad?"

She paused.

"No," she said after a moment. "You were born to go.

"But I missed so many years," he replied, looking down. "I wasn't here for Durga Pujas. For your surgery. For Baba's retirement. I couldn't even make it for Dadu's funeral."

She looked at him, her voice calm.

"Yes, you missed some years. But we never missed you."

Arnab looked up, puzzled.

She smiled.

"We carried you in everything. Your photo on the wall. Your name in every prayer. When we made your favourite rice pudding on your birthday. You weren't missing. You were… *incomplete.*"

That hit him hard.

More than any reproach would have.

He walked out and sat beneath the mango tree.

The sunlight filtered through the leaves in fractured patterns, landing on his face like blessings from above.

He felt the ground with his palms. It was dry, cracked in places, but alive.

He had walked so far from his roots that he had begun to doubt they were still there.

But they were.

They had never judged him.

They had simply waited.

Around noon, a few villagers came by to see him again. Tapan Da brought a hand-woven bamboo basket. Ranu Didi dropped off some homemade pickles. Even the Pradhan's assistant came by with folded hands and spoke of the Panchayat's admiration for "Ashapur's foreign-returned son."

Arnab listened politely, smiled when he needed to, but stayed mostly quiet.

Because now, more than ever, he realized—this village didn't see him for his job title.

They didn't know about his corporate collapse.

They didn't know that he had been silently fired, his emails cut off, his keycards revoked. That his badge had stopped working and no one from his company had even called.

They didn't know he had stood outside his office building one last time before leaving the US, holding a cardboard box of leftover memories.

Here, none of that mattered.

Here, he was not a designation.

He was *Arnab*.

The postmaster's son.

That afternoon, he lay on the charpai under the veranda.

The sky turned heavy with monsoon clouds.

Thunder rumbled far off.

He closed his eyes.

And for a fleeting moment, imagined **Rhea** sitting beside him. Her hand in his. Her belly swollen with the promise of life. Her laughter bouncing off the old walls.

He didn't open his eyes.

He let the vision fade softly, like a curtain being drawn in slow motion.

Not forgotten.

Just… resting.

Before dusk, Seema came to him with a fresh set of clothes.

"Wear this tomorrow," she said. "You're going to the temple with us."

Arnab nodded.

He folded the clothes carefully and placed them on his bed.

Then, turning to her, asked:

"Ma… if I wanted to stay here for some time. Not just visit. Would you… would you mind?"

She looked up sharply.

Then smiled.

"We have no room for minding. Only room for keeping."

He didn't need more words than that.

He didn't even need a plan yet.

He just needed to be here.

That night, after dinner, Arnab stood at the doorway.

His father joined him, both looking out at the dark lane ahead.

"Things are changing," Gourango said.

"Yes," Arnab replied.

"Some changes come from the outside," his father continued. "Some from inside. The hard ones… they start inside."

Arnab didn't respond immediately.

Then he said, "I think something inside me is finally ready."

"Good," Gourango said. "Because the world won't wait for long."

Arnab turned to him. "But roots… they wait, don't they?"

His father placed a hand on his shoulder.

"Roots don't judge, son. They hold."

And in that sentence was everything Arnab had needed to hear.

Chapter 3: The Boy Who Went Too Far

Part 1 of 5 – Mango Trees and Marbles

There's something about childhood that never quite dies in a village like Ashapur. The red soil holds footprints longer than any road ever built. Trees remember names carved into bark. Wells echo laughter from decades ago.

For Arnab Chatterjee, it began under a mango tree.

A crooked one, to be precise, leaning left like an old man peering over a gate. That tree, in the backyard of their modest government quarters, was his fortress, his hiding spot, his dream-catcher. Its branches had once hosted paper kites, chameleons, and at least one stolen exam paper—safely hidden during his class 3 "Great Escape Plan".

That was Arnab: not naughty, but always curious. Not rebellious, but quietly defiant. He would ask "why" more than "how", and he would often answer it himself before anyone had a chance to respond.

A Marble for a Memory

At six years old, Arnab had a peculiar obsession with marbles.

Not the toy itself, but what they *contained*—those swirling patterns of glass and colour that reminded him of galaxies. He believed, with unshakable conviction, that each marble held a tiny world.

He kept them in an old Horlicks jar under his bed—organized by colour and size, labelled with homemade paper tags. "Neel Tara", "Agun Lok", "Dhusor Brikkho"—names no one else understood.

Dulal understood, though.

Dulal was Arnab's first and best friend. A lanky boy with dimples and an endless appetite for mangoes and mischief, Dulal was the yang to Arnab's yin.

While Arnab read books and built paper circuits, Dulal climbed trees, stole pickles from neighbours' kitchens, and learned how to catch fish with his bare hands.

They were inseparable. One with dirt under his nails, the other with ink stains on his fingers.

Mornings at the Post Office Gate

Arnab's house stood just behind the Ashapur Post Office, where his father, Gourango Chatterjee, ruled with an iron stamp.

Every morning at 7:30 sharp, Arnab would hear the familiar whistle of his father walking past the courtyard.

It wasn't an aggressive call—more like a ritual. One short whistle, followed by the soft jingle of his bicycle bell.

Sometimes Arnab would race out, his satchel swinging from one shoulder, shoes half-tied, and fall into pace beside his father as he walked the fifty-odd meters to the post office gate.

"I'll take the corner bench and read today," he'd declare.

"Not before finishing multiplication tables," Gourango would reply without looking.

Ma—Seema Devi—would scold from the kitchen doorway, "And you'll eat your banana before school, or I'll tell your master you're fainting in class again!"

This was their morning song—off-key but harmonious in its own way.

The Boy Who Always Asked Too Much

Arnab wasn't easy to handle.

He didn't like easy answers. If someone said "Because I said so," Arnab would stare back until they said more.

In class 4, he stopped speaking to his science teacher for two days because she said "Air is everywhere," and when he asked "Then how do fish breathe underwater?", she told him not to interrupt the syllabus.

He brought a fish to school the next day—in a plastic bottle—and asked her again.

His parents were called in.

"You should've seen his face," Gourango told the headmaster. "Proud. Not defiant. Just… wanting to know."

They laughed it off then, but Seema worried.

"Is he too different?" she asked one night while folding laundry. "Too dreamy?"

Gourango only said, "The world needs those who dream first. Let's just keep his feet grounded till his wings are strong."

Dulal's Slingshot and Arnab's First Real Lesson

One day, in summer, Dulal shot a crow with a slingshot.

It had been a perfect shot—straight through the air, striking the bird as it sat on the post office wall.

The bird fluttered violently and fell. The boys rushed over.

Arnab froze.

The crow twitched once. Then stopped.

He stood still, chest heaving, tears brimming.

Dulal looked confused. "What happened? It's just a crow."

Arnab didn't speak. He picked up the bird with trembling hands, placed it gently under the shade of the neem tree, and sat beside it in silence.

That evening, he didn't speak to Dulal.

The next morning, he buried the crow and placed one of his favourite marbles on top of the tiny grave—a deep blue one he called "Jol Tara".

When Dulal tried to apologize, Arnab only said, "We shouldn't break what we didn't make."

Dulal never used the slingshot again.

The Rain That Changed Everything

During Arnab's tenth year, Ashapur saw one of its worst monsoons in decades.

Water filled the streets. Frogs croaked from inside slippers. The post office was closed for a week due to flooding. Their house leaked in three corners of the ceiling.

Arnab and Dulal, cooped up indoors, built a raft from bamboo sticks, plastic bottles, and leftover rope.

When the rain paused, they launched it on the flooded pathway outside.

It floated.

It was *magic*.

For ten minutes, they took turns pretending to be explorers in a drowned city.

Then the raft hit a rock, cracked, and sunk slowly.

Arnab stared at it for a long time.

"Don't worry," Dulal said. "We'll build a bigger one."

Arnab nodded, but something had shifted.

It was his first experience of watching a dream break in silence.

No drama. No warning.

Just a soft, inevitable sinking.

His Father's Umbrella and the First Big Words

One afternoon, soaked after school, Arnab came home shivering. His umbrella had broken. His uniform clung to his skin like wet tissue.

His father came home around the same time, equally drenched, with only his post office satchel dry under a makeshift plastic cover.

They sat under the eaves, dripping together.

"Why didn't you bring your big umbrella, Baba?" Arnab asked.

"It's old. I gave it to the new postman. His tore."

"But yours was better."

"Yes," Gourango said, pulling the satchel close. "But some things are better shared when needed."

That moment stayed with Arnab longer than any school lesson.

The Library That Wasn't

Ashapur didn't have a library.

So Arnab built one in his mind.

Every evening, he'd sit on the roof with his books—a worn copy of *Discovering India*, translated Tagore poems, and a science encyclopaedia with missing pages—and imagine rows of shelves, hundreds of spines, a desk where people signed their names to borrow stories.

One day, he found an old biscuit tin, wrote "Ashapur Public Library" on the lid, and started lending out his books.

Dulal borrowed a comic book.

Murari Kaka borrowed a Bengali detective novel.

Even the Pradhan's wife took a cookbook once.

For two years, that biscuit tin became the library registry. Until he left for the city.

When he came back, the tin was gone.

But Ranu Didi still had his copy of *Jules Verne* in her tea stall drawer, protected in plastic.

The Seeds Were Already Sown

By the time Arnab reached class 8, teachers whispered about scholarships.

Gourango started researching schools in Kolkata.

Seema began quietly saving money in biscuit tins and sewing blouse linings.

Arnab didn't know what future waited.

He only knew he wanted to build things—machines, models, ideas.

He wanted to learn everything, then teach others.

He told Dulal once, under the mango tree, "I want to go where the roads never end."

Dulal replied, "I want to build a shop on the road you leave behind."

They laughed.

But they were both right.

And neither knew how far that road would stretch.

Part 2 of 5 – Classrooms and Kites

Ashapur's mornings always carried a kind of freshness that clung to your senses—a chill that hugged your ankles, the earthy smell of cow dung cakes drying on walls, and the comforting crackle of someone lighting a coal stove in a nearby hut.

By the time Arnab entered middle school, his world had begun expanding beyond the mango trees and marble jars. And yet, certain things stayed sacred—like the **annual kite-flying contest** that turned the skies over Ashapur into a battlefield of colour, string, and pride.

The Boy Who Loved the Sky

Arnab had learned to fly kites from his grandfather—an old man with the gait of a retired soldier and the voice of a lullaby. They used to sit on the terrace, kites spread like wounded birds between them, while the old man would explain the science of the sky.

"Don't pull too fast. Feel the wind first. A kite is not a fight—it's a friendship."

Arnab remembered those words every time he stood on the rooftop of his house, fingers wrapped around the spool, eyes squinting upward as his kite—bright orange, with a silver tail—danced its way higher.

Dulal, of course, took a more aggressive approach.

He liked the loud-coloured ones. Pink, yellow, black—with sharp threads coated in crushed glass (*manja*). His kites were warriors, not dancers.

"You go for peace," Dulal would say, laughing. "I go for victory."

But even when Dulal's kite sliced through the sky like a missile and cut down two others in a row, it was Arnab's that stayed longer.

Grace, not aggression.

Patience, not pressure.

A lesson he would forget years later. But in those days, it defined him.

The Classrooms That Shaped Him

Ashapur High School was a yellow building with three classrooms, two broken fans, and one shared blackboard.

Arnab sat in the front row of class 6, back straight, notebooks spotless. He had a reputation—not of being the loudest, or even the smartest—but the most *curious*.

He asked questions that unnerved teachers.

"Why do we only salute the flag and not the Constitution?"

"If the sun is a star, does it mean our sky is already night and day at once?"

"Why are girls told to sit in the back row?"

Some teachers appreciated his inquiries. Others rolled their eyes.

One day, the math teacher locked him out for correcting a mistake on the board too confidently.

Arnab stood in the corridor, back to the wall, arms crossed. He didn't cry. He didn't argue.

When his father heard, he visited the school the next morning—not to scold the teacher, but to tell his son:

"Next time, ask the question. Then wait for the space to answer it."

The First Crush and the Red Ribbon

Her name was **Rikta**.

She sat two benches ahead of Arnab. Hair always braided in two neat plaits. A red ribbon tied at the end of each. She smelled like eucalyptus and borrowed books from the library more than anyone else.

Arnab didn't know what to call what he felt.

He only knew that on days she didn't come to school, the class felt… dimmer.

Once, when Rikta lost her pencil box, Arnab found it during recess. Instead of returning it directly, he placed it on her desk with a note folded inside:

"Everyone notices when you're not here. – A"

He never signed his name. But Rikta smiled in his direction that day.

Years later, Arnab would recall that moment not as love, but as **a lesson in appreciation**. In recognizing beauty and kindness quietly, without expectation.

The Science Fair That Almost Wasn't

In class 8, a regional science exhibition was announced. Each school could nominate only one project.

Arnab's idea was simple: a low-cost water purifier using charcoal, sand, and boiled cloth mesh. He had built a prototype in his courtyard, using discarded buckets and leftover plumbing pipes.

It worked.

Word spread.

He was selected to represent the school.

But what he didn't know—what came out later—was that **his best friend Dulal had submitted the same idea**, two days earlier.

Dulal never mentioned it. Never accused. Never confronted.

Arnab found out from another student.

Crushed with guilt, Arnab approached him during lunch break.

"Why didn't you say something?"

Dulal shrugged. "Because yours worked better."

"But it was your idea."

"We've shared ideas since we were six," Dulal said, chewing on a stick of sugarcane. "Let this one be yours."

Arnab tried to back out of the fair, but Dulal wouldn't let him.

"Go make the village proud. That's all I want."

And he did.

Arnab's project won first place.

Ashapur's name was printed in *Pratidin* newspaper. The school headmaster wept openly. Gourango bought an extra copy to frame.

But Arnab never forgot.

Not the victory.

Not the sacrifice.

Board Exams and the Fight

Class 10 changed everything.

The pressure. The expectations. The tutoring.

Gourango, once gentle in tone, now became a strict monitor of every hour.

Seema Devi brought food to his table, but stopped asking if he'd had enough sleep.

Even Dulal, though still playful, began disappearing for longer hours, helping his father with their cycle repair shop.

Tensions built. Arnab snapped easily. Once, he yelled at Dulal for playing cricket too loud near the house.

"Some of us have real futures to prepare for!" he had shouted.

Dulal had gone silent.

Didn't speak for a week.

When he finally came back, he didn't bring sugarcane or marbles.

He brought silence.

The Letter That Changed His World

A white envelope arrived one morning, bearing the seal of a national scholarship program. Arnab opened it with trembling hands.

He had won.

Full scholarship to a prestigious pre-engineering program in Kolkata.

Gourango didn't speak for a full minute after reading it.

Then he walked out, stood in the sun, and quietly cried.

Seema Devi hugged him that night with such force, Arnab could barely breathe.

But Dulal said only one thing:

"You better not forget where you learned to tie kite strings."

Arnab had laughed then.

But deep down, he felt a ripple of fear.

That life was **pulling him away**.

That the string was tightening.

And soon… it might snap.

Part 3 of 5 – Letters, Loans, and Goodbyes

The envelope that carried Arnab's scholarship results wasn't just a letter—it was a storm, quiet and unfolding, in the lives of the Chatterjee family.

The moment it was opened, the axis of the house shifted. The air around the breakfast table felt different. Even the almirah in the living room, where old documents slept, stood a little taller as if it knew one of its own would now sit in a place of national importance.

Arnab's name would be known—not just within Ashapur's red-soil borders, but in classrooms where the language of ambition was spoken fluently.

But pride… it has a cost.

A Home that Gave All It Had

That evening, the house buzzed with visitors. Relatives from nearby villages, neighbours, school teachers—all came bearing sweets, flowers, blessings, and unsolicited advice.

"Ami bolchilam. E bachcha tar kichu to ache," said Murari Kaka, gleaming with half-pride and half-credit.

"He'll go far. Just like that boy from Medinipur who now teaches in Canada."

"Will he come back? Will he forget this village?"

Through it all, Arnab sat quietly in the corner, not knowing whether to smile or bow or hide.

Inside the kitchen, Seema Devi counted her savings—not aloud, not with hope, but with exactitude.

Her blouse lining, stitched thicker over the years, now unfolded to reveal ten crumpled notes and a few coins.

"Gold?" she asked Gourango.

He shook his head.

"No, not yet."

"But for the visa process…?"

He lit the lantern silently.

They both knew.

The scholarship covered tuition. Not flight tickets. Not living expenses. Not the documentation charges or passport or the endless hidden fees that people only whispered about in passing.

Gourango went to bed that night and didn't sleep.

He stared at the ceiling, hands folded behind his head, calculating a way to send his only son to a life he had only heard of on All India Radio.

The Loan and the Letter

A week later, Gourango pawned the last bit of his father's land rights—ancestral plots that were meant to be passed down.

He did it without flinching.

Seema sold her wedding bangles to a friend, not for market value, but for **urgency**.

The bank official came home personally—out of respect, and perhaps guilt.

"It's not much," he said, handing over the envelope. "But it's enough for a start."

Arnab stood near the door that day, watching the papers being signed.

He didn't interrupt.

He just stood—guilt pounding like waves in his chest.

Later that night, he quietly crept into his parents' room.

They were awake. They always were now.

"I can wait one more year," he said. "We can save more. Maybe I can go after that."

Seema turned in her bed.

"No."

"You don't understand. It's okay, Ma. I don't have to go now."

"You'll go," said Gourango firmly.

"But what if—"

Gourango sat up.

"You'll go, Arnab. You'll fly. Even if it means we walk the rest of our lives."

That ended the argument.

The Village That Raised Him

In the days that followed, Ashapur turned into a celebration.

Posters appeared on trees.

"Proud of Our Son – Arnab Chatterjee, Selected for International Science Program"

A public function was held in the school courtyard. The headmaster gave a speech longer than necessary. Rikta smiled from the audience. Dulal clapped the loudest.

Arnab was gifted a watch. It ticked three minutes slow, but it meant everything.

Dulal gave him a coin.

"Lucky one," he said. "My father found it near the pond the day I was born. It's older than both of us."

Arnab took it like it was currency from another realm.

"I'll return it," he promised.

Dulal smirked. "Only if you forget your accent."

The Goodbye That Shook Them All

The day of his departure came too soon.

The train to Kolkata left at 5:45 AM. Arnab was packed, nervous, and silent.

His suitcase was small. His dreams were not.

Seema wept quietly into her sari, fingers brushing his forehead again and again.

"You will call?"

"Every week, Ma."

"Eat properly?"

"Yes."

"And don't forget your roots."

"I won't."

Gourango stood by the door. He didn't touch his son, didn't speak.

Only when the taxi engine started, he stepped forward and placed his hand on Arnab's shoulder.

"Don't come back until you've made something of yourself."

Arnab nodded.

"Baba…"

"I'll wait."

The taxi turned the corner.

And the house behind him—where he had built rocket models, read under a dim lamp, and once cried because he failed a Bengali dictation test—grew smaller and smaller.

Until it disappeared.

First Touch with the Foreign World

At the airport in Kolkata, Arnab felt like a fish on land.

His tongue dried up. His palms sweated. Everything felt too bright. Too fast.

When he boarded the international flight, he couldn't stop shaking.

The seatbelt sign blinked.

And he gripped the coin Dulal had given him, whispering to himself:

"This is it. This is where you change."

He didn't cry.

But as the aircraft lifted off, he looked down at the land.

The rivers. The fields. The houses.

And thought:

"I'm leaving more than geography behind."

Part 4 of 5 – From Dreams to Distance

Change doesn't happen with a bang. It comes quietly—an accumulation of adjustments, compromises, and distances you tell yourself are temporary… until one day, they aren't.

When Arnab first stepped into the campus of the pre-engineering institute in Kolkata, it felt like a movie set.

Tall buildings, freshly painted. A canteen that served cold coffee in glass mugs. A library with working air-conditioning and leather chairs. Students from Delhi, Bangalore, Ahmedabad. Conversations in English sprinkled with tech jargon and ambition.

For the first week, Arnab barely spoke. He watched, listened, calculated the tone, the rhythm, the rules of this new world.

He stopped using the word *Ma* when talking to others.

Started calling home "the village."

And when someone asked where he was from, he would say, "West Bengal. Near Midnapore," not "Ashapur."

Learning the Language of Aspiration

Arnab wasn't the smartest in his batch.

He was among the quiet ones—observing more than asserting.

But he had something most of them didn't: **fire in his belly**, born not out of privilege, but sacrifice.

Every exam he passed wasn't just a personal win—it was a repayment.

Of a pawned gold bangle.

Of sleepless nights where Ma kept the lantern burning until he returned her call.

Of a village that watched the sky at night, whispering prayers that their son make it to the moon.

He studied relentlessly.

He aced physics. Struggled in computer science initially. Got a C in his first data structures lab.

And then stayed up three nights in a row until he understood why pointers mattered more than grades.

The First Laptop and the First Apartment

When Arnab received his first internship stipend from a small AI startup during his second year, he did not spend it on pizza or sneakers like the others.

He bought a second-hand **Dell Inspiron**.

With scratches on the lid, a fading keypad, and a sticker on the corner that read *Property of IIT Techfest 2015*.

That laptop became his best friend.

He named it **"Jol Tara"**—the same name he had given one of his favourite marbles back in Ashapur.

At night, when the hostel slept, he wrote code.

Neural nets. Logistic regression models. Even a small Bengali OCR script that could scan handwritten post office entries.

No one knew about that script.

Not yet.

Rhea

She came into his life like a well-written function—precise, purposeful, and quietly powerful.

Rhea was from Mumbai. Confident. Fluent in sarcasm and software.

They met during a group project on "AI for Rural Systems."

Arnab suggested they build a basic digital tracking system for small post offices.

Rhea raised an eyebrow. "That's oddly specific."

"It's what I know," he replied.

They ended up working till 4 a.m. every day for two weeks. Arguing over logic flows. Drinking cheap coffee. Laughing over code comments.

She once told him, "You've got roots deeper than most people have feet."

He didn't understand it then.

He would later.

The Call That Didn't Happen

On the night of his father's 60th birthday, Arnab was supposed to call at 7:30 PM sharp.

Seema had prepared his father's favourite sweets. Gourango had put on the kurta Arnab had couriered last year.

The village was invited for tea and snacks. The neighbours asked when the "foreign-returned" son would join via video.

At 7:20 PM, Arnab was caught in a debugging spiral with his project team.

At 7:45, his phone buzzed—six missed calls from Ma.

At 8:30, he remembered.

By then, it was too late.

He messaged:

"Sorry Ma. Got stuck in lab. Hug Baba from me."

She replied an hour later:

"He went to sleep."

No anger. No drama.

Just distance.

One that would take years to measure.

Success and the Silence It Brings

Arnab graduated with distinction. Received three job offers. Chose the one that paid the least but let him work on neural efficiency models.

He moved to **Bangalore**, then **San Francisco**, as part of an internal mobility program.

His apartment in Palo Alto overlooked a row of designer homes.

His kitchen had a smart fridge that ordered groceries when the milk ran out.

His watch buzzed with reminders to breathe.

He bought a car with heated seats.

And he stopped calling home regularly.

Not because he didn't care.

But because the **gap between his world and theirs** had grown so wide, he didn't know how to cross it anymore.

When Seema asked him on a call if the rice cooker was still working, he told her he ate quinoa now.

When Gourango asked if post offices in America still used paper, he said, "They barely use people."

And he felt the silence that followed.

The Festival of Disconnect

One year, during Durga Puja, the villagers built a pandal shaped like a post box.

In the centre, a small clay idol of **Arnab working at a computer** was placed beside Maa Durga.

He saw the photo on Facebook—posted by his school friend Tapan.

Under it, the caption read:
"Ashapur's own tech god. He's taking Bengal to the world."

Arnab stared at the image for a long time.

Then closed the app.

He didn't know whether to feel honoured or ashamed.

The Price of Progress

Years passed.

He became Head of AI at **NextGenCorp**.

He led a team of sixty-five.

He gave TED-style talks, shook hands with CEOs, mentored interns, and held boardroom discussions about "ethical automation frameworks for lean delivery chains."

And with every automation module, someone's job became redundant.

He knew it.

He told himself he was building systems that were smarter, faster, more scalable.

He told himself he wasn't taking away jobs—just eliminating inefficiencies.

But at night, when he turned off his screens, he sometimes saw his father's desk.

The stamp pad.

The ink-stained fingers.

The woman who needed help writing her pension form.

And he wondered…

Was this the future they prayed for?

Part 5 of 5 – Return of the Stranger

By the time Arnab's flight touched down at Kolkata airport, it had been **eighteen years** since he last stood on the soil of Ashapur. Yet the strange thing was—not the foreignness of the place—but the **foreignness of himself**.

He wasn't the boy who built bamboo rafts with Dulal anymore.

He wasn't the boy who believed marbles held galaxies, or that filling out post office forms was a sacred task.

He had become… something else.

A sum of systems. A man made of routine, regret, and revenue dashboards.

But the village had waited.

And it hadn't changed its language.

It still spoke in whispers of rain.

In smells of rice soaked in mustard oil.

In the squeak of a hand pump and the rustle of banana leaves.

In **roots**.

The House That Still Knew His Name

Back in his childhood room, Arnab sat at the desk where he had once drawn blueprints for model rockets. The desk was older now, a bit cracked near the edges, but it still had the mark he had carved: "A.C. 98".

He ran his finger over it slowly.

Dust clung to his skin, as if remembering him.

On the shelf, his books still lived—yellowing, dog-eared, survivors of monsoons and mice.

In a tin box under the bed, the old Horlicks jar of marbles remained. Not all of them were there. A few were cracked. But inside were still the blue one, the green swirl, the milky white.

He held one up to the light.

"Jol Tara."

He whispered the name without thinking.

He didn't cry.

But something inside him folded.

Softly.

Like an origami kite being pressed into an envelope of memory.

Ashapur Through New Eyes

Walking through the village as a grown man was a surreal experience.

Everything felt smaller. Not in stature, but in **urgency**.

The well he once feared falling into now barely reached his waist.

The banyan tree where Dulal used to climb with a rope swing now looked like it bent with time.

Even the school compound—where once he thought the world began and ended—was just a yellow box of fading promise.

And yet… **the people** remained.

Tapan Da still repaired cycles, though now his son helped him.

Ranu Didi still ran her tea stall, with a new shade cloth and her grandson as delivery boy.

Even Murari Kaka—half-blind and fully opinionated—sat by the temple wall, greeting everyone like a judge overseeing a kingdom of mud paths and banana trees.

When he saw Arnab, he raised a shaky hand.

"Postmaster Babu's son."

Arnab smiled. "Still saying that?"

"What else should I say?" the old man replied. "You may have left. But your name didn't."

Dulal

Arnab found him near the market road, fixing a puncture in a boy's cycle.

Same lean frame, though older now. Tanned. Slight limp.

Their eyes met.

No drama. No overjoyed hugs.

Just a handshake.

"Bujhtei parini tui ashbi." *(Didn't think you'd actually come.)*

"Neither did I," Arnab replied.

They sat together for hours that evening, on a low boundary wall, drinking tea from clay cups.

They didn't speak about the past too much.

But at one point, Arnab pulled something from his pocket.

The **coin**.

"I kept it."

Dulal didn't react.

"Thought I'd lost it once, during a blizzard. But I found it in my sock drawer a week before I flew back."

Dulal took it. Turned it in his fingers.

Then returned it.

"You'll need it again."

Rediscovering the Soil

Arnab began to rise early.

Took morning walks along the pond. Fed stray dogs leftover biscuits. Sat on the terrace after lunch and read through his father's old documents.

At first, he felt like a tourist.

Then… something shifted.

He began to **notice**.

The way children still wrote letters on lined paper.

The way the temple priest double-checked money orders before blessing them.

The way Seema kept his clothes folded the same way she had when he was ten.

And slowly, the alien began to become familiar.

Not because the place changed.

But because **he stopped resisting** it.

The Moment It All Mattered

One evening, as the sun dipped behind the palm trees, casting long golden shadows across the courtyard, Arnab stood beside the post office.

His fingers brushed against the iron red letterbox.

And he remembered something his father once said:

"We don't just deliver letters, Arnab. We deliver faith. Someone, somewhere, always waits at the other end."

That night, he opened his laptop for the first time in days.

Not to check email.

Not to submit a report.

But to write.

A proposal.

A dream.

A blueprint.

To **digitize rural post offices** using a model that wouldn't eliminate jobs, but repurpose them.

Retrain the staff.

Make postmen digital navigators, not obsolete messengers.

To let villages like Ashapur have both roots and upgrades.

The Stranger Who Belonged

Arnab wasn't fully healed.

Not yet.

He still had memories that ached. Still had corners in his mind where silence echoed too loudly.

But in the long afternoons, when he helped his father arrange registers, or when he walked barefoot to the tea stall, or when he smiled at a child playing with a marble…

He felt a little more complete.

Not the boy who left.

Not the man who conquered.

Just… Arnab.

Someone who had finally found the balance between what he was and what he had become.

Someone who had travelled the world, only to find **home** was never on a map.

Chapter 4: When Sparks Ignite

Part 1 of 5 – A Meeting Written by Fate

The San Francisco evening sky shimmered with a thousand corporate dreams. Downtown lights blinked from chrome towers, and self-driving taxis whirred past glass-fronted cafés. It was a city of ideas, startups, and sleepless ambition—a city Arnab Chatterjee had conquered, or so he thought.

That evening, like every other weekday, Arnab left the **NextGenCorp** headquarters carrying the invisible exhaustion of a man whose life was ruled by slides, dashboards, and endless emails. His white Tesla Model 3 awaited him in the underground parking lot, neatly slotted between two EV-only charging stations.

But something was off.

The Breakdown

Arnab slid into the driver's seat, pressed the ignition, and frowned.

The car hummed once.

Then nothing.

A yellow notification blinked on the dash:

"Charging Error Detected. Consult Manual."

He sighed.

He wasn't in the mood for manuals.

Thirty-six straight hours of code reviews and pilot launches had drained even his legendary stamina.

He got out, inspecting the charging socket. It looked fine—at least to the naked eye.

He tried rebooting the system.

Nothing.

The automated assistant chirped politely, "Charging failure due to possible obstruction. Please check connection."

Arnab muttered a string of Bengali curses under his breath. The high-end tech he had once worshipped was now mocking him.

Finally, frustrated, he tapped open the **SOS app** to call a support technician.

That's when he heard footsteps.

A Spark, Literally

A young woman—mid-twenties, jeans and a maroon Stanford hoodie—was crouched near the adjacent parking bay, gathering her backpack.

She looked up and caught his eye.

Wide, almond-shaped eyes, gleaming with curiosity.

"Trouble?" she asked, tilting her head.

Arnab hesitated. He wasn't exactly feeling chatty.

"Yes. EV's dead."

She slung the backpack over one shoulder and walked toward him.

"Mind if I take a look? I used to do field tests for Tesla interns."

Arnab raised an eyebrow. "You're an intern at Tesla?"

She laughed. "Was. Now interning at NextGenCorp. Rhea—new AI division."

She extended her hand.

Arnab shook it automatically, feeling a strange jolt of warmth.

The Fixer

Without waiting for permission, Rhea crouched near the charging socket.

"You tried rebooting, I assume?" she said, her fingers tracing the outlines carefully.

"Of course," Arnab muttered.

She clicked her tongue. "Smart guy. But sometimes it's the dumb things that break smart systems."

Pulling out a wooden chopstick from her coffee cup holder—God knows why she had it—she gently prodded into the socket.

Arnab winced.

"This is a precision component!"

She winked. "So is a jammed ballpoint pen. Doesn't mean you replace it when it's stuck."

After a few delicate taps, a tiny piece of plastic debris—no bigger than a rice grain—dislodged.

The car blinked to life.

Charging resumed.

A Different Kind of Charge

Arnab stared.

"How did you even think of that?"

She grinned, brushing her hair behind her ear. "Design thinking, my friend. Systems fail at their weakest junctions, not their strongest."

He couldn't help but smile.

It wasn't just her cleverness—it was her energy. Her refusal to be impressed by titles or tech.

"Can I buy you a coffee?" he asked, half-joking, half-serious.

She tilted her head again, mock-serious.

"Only if it's a strong filter coffee. I'm Bengali, remember? We judge caffeine like others judge wine."

He laughed, genuinely this time.

For the first time in months, **something inside him felt unstuck.**

The First Coffee

They walked across the street to a small café tucked behind a glass art gallery.

No suits. No slide decks. No KPIs.

Just two people.

Two lives beginning to find an unexpected intersection.

Rhea spoke in bursts—about her research on AI ethics, her childhood summers in Kolkata, her love for Rabindra Sangeet and indie punk music, her obsession with origami and hackathons.

Arnab listened, fascinated.

He realized he had forgotten what **unfiltered enthusiasm** sounded like.

When they finished coffee, he said, almost shyly, "Do you want to grab dinner next week?"

She grinned.

"No."

He blinked.

She laughed at his expression.

"I'm free tomorrow night. Why wait?"

Part 2 of 5 – Sparks into Fire

The next evening, Arnab found himself standing outside a cozy Indian restaurant on Valencia Street, nervously adjusting the cuffs of his shirt. It wasn't like him to be jittery before a casual dinner, but Rhea's energy had disrupted the predictability of his meticulously organized life—and he wasn't sure if he hated it or craved more of it.

When she arrived—wearing a simple mustard yellow kurta over jeans, her hair tied in a loose braid—he realized he had no control over the outcome.

He was already falling.

The Dinner That Wasn't Just Dinner

Over plates of kosha mangsho and luchi, Rhea peppered him with questions.

"Did you always want to be an AI engineer?"

"Not exactly," Arnab chuckled. "I wanted to be a postman once."

"A postman?" she laughed, almost dropping her fork.

He nodded, smiling at the memory. "In my village, the postman was like a magician. He brought stories, news, hope. As a kid, it seemed heroic."

She leaned closer. "Maybe you still are a postman. Just delivering different kinds of messages."

He looked at her, startled by the simplicity and depth of her observation.

Conversations Like Tides

They talked for hours.

About technology and loneliness.

About identity and exile.

About the immigrant hunger for belonging.

When the restaurant closed for the night, they wandered down the fog-slick streets, two shadows under a misty moon, their voices weaving a tapestry between lampposts.

Rhea told him about her scholarship struggles, about how coding gave her freedom when money couldn't, about how she hated pumpkin spice lattes but loved jalebi dipped in cold milk.

Arnab told her about Ashapur, about the monsoon rains that flooded the football field, about his father's ink-stained fingers and his mother's butter-soft rotis.

By the time they parted, something irreversible had shifted between them.

The Small Rituals

It became a pattern.

Coffee after work.

Walks by the pier.

Arguments over the best Rosogolla shop in Kolkata.

Silly fights about cricket vs. baseball.

Once, during a hackathon, they both pulled all-nighters—not for prizes, but just to see whose chatbot could tell better Bengali jokes.

He brought her mishti doi from the only decent Indian grocery store. She stuck Post-it notes with bad puns inside his laptop sleeve.

Their connection wasn't cinematic.

It was **organic**.

Like a creeper plant finding sunlight through narrow concrete cracks.

First Signs of Something Deeper

One evening, after a particularly brutal client meeting where Arnab was publicly criticized for a design flaw that wasn't his fault, he sat slumped in the office cafeteria, pretending to read his laptop screen.

Rhea slid into the chair across from him.

No words.

Just her hand, sliding a chocolate bar across the table.

"Emergency medicine," she said softly.

He looked up, and in that look, something vulnerable flickered open.

He didn't thank her.

He didn't need to.

Some silences said more than paragraphs.

A Night to Remember

It was after a weekend road trip to Half Moon Bay that Arnab finally admitted it—to himself, if not aloud.

They had spent the day laughing over terrible car karaoke, arguing over the right way to eat pani puri, and daring each other to run barefoot on the icy sand.

As they sat by a bonfire that evening, wrapped in borrowed blankets, he realized—

He could see every tomorrow with her.

She turned her head, catching him staring.

"What?" she smiled, teeth white against the firelight.

He shook his head, laughing under his breath.

"Nothing."

Everything.

The Proposal That Wasn't Planned

There was no grand gesture.

No ring hidden in dessert.

No rose petals spelling out "Marry Me."

One night, while washing dishes in Rhea's tiny studio apartment, elbow-deep in soap suds and laughter, Arnab turned to her and said:

"We should get married."

She paused, mid-scrub.

Looked at him.

"Is that a proposal or a panic attack?"

He grinned. "A proposal. Definitely."

She laughed—a bright, bell-like laugh that made the tiny kitchen feel like a universe.

"Okay," she said simply, flicking a soap bubble at him.

"Okay?" he echoed, stunned.

"Okay," she repeated, throwing her arms around his neck.

The Simplicity of It

They didn't announce it with Instagram posts.

They didn't shop for diamonds.

They didn't draw up elaborate plans.

They just decided—like how some trees decide when it's time to bloom.

And in that quiet decision, a new life began.

One neither of them could have known would be so achingly short—and yet, so infinitely complete.

Part 3 of 5 – Building a World Together

Their wedding was so small it barely qualified as one.

A courthouse in downtown San Mateo. A borrowed white dress from Rhea's roommate. A hastily rented navy-blue blazer for Arnab from a second-hand boutique.

Witnesses?
A Gujarati Uber driver who insisted on blessing them with tilak from a tube of red lipstick.
A Filipina secretary from NextGenCorp who cried harder than Rhea's own mother on the video call.

Vows were whispered more than spoken.

Promises were scribbled on sticky notes stuck to their fridge.

Yet if love was measured in authenticity, **theirs could have filled cathedrals**.

Their First Home

They moved into a modest two-bedroom apartment in Sunnyvale.

Second floor. No elevator. View of the parking lot.

The walls were bare, but the windows caught the sunset just right.

They spent their weekends scouring flea markets for furniture, giggling over crooked table legs and wobbly chairs.

Rhea insisted on a tiny balcony garden, even though Arnab warned her they'd probably kill everything.

They didn't.

The basil thrived.

So did they.

Work, Dreams, and Shared Struggles

They both worked brutal hours.

Deadlines loomed like mountains.

Prototype failures. Executive tantrums. 14-hour hackathons fueled by cold pizza and flat Coke.

Sometimes they fought.

Over Rhea staying late at field tests.

Over Arnab's stubbornness about corporate politics.

Over whether shukto or aloo posto deserved to be called the 'King of Bengali Food.'

But every fight ended the same way.

Two spoons clinking inside a shared tub of ice cream.

Two exhausted heads leaning against each other on the living room floor, TV playing something neither was watching.

Dreams They Sketched on Napkins

They dreamed like immigrants do—with both awe and terror.

Of buying a fixer-upper house someday.

Of visiting Santiniketan together during Poush Mela.

Of starting a consulting firm focused on ethical AI.

Of maybe—just maybe—having a baby who would speak Bengali before English.

They wrote some of these dreams on scraps of napkin paper.

Arnab kept them all inside an old watch box.

Hidden.

Sacred.

The Baby News

It was a Saturday morning, fog rolling in thick over the bay.

Rhea barged into the bathroom holding a pregnancy test.

He had toothpaste in his mouth when she screamed, "DUDE, WE'RE HAVING A BABY!"

Arnab almost choked on the foam.

He stared at the two pink lines, blinking like an idiot.

Rhea beamed, hopping around the bathroom tiles in pure, unfiltered joy.

He spat the toothpaste, grabbed her face with both hands, and kissed her forehead.

"Best bug report I ever got," he whispered.

She laughed until she cried.

Planning for Tomorrow

They bought tiny onesies online.

They argued about names—Rhea preferring poetic ones like "Anaya" or "Ishaan," Arnab secretly leaning toward traditional ones like "Abir" or "Madhurima."

They discussed whether they'd move to a slightly bigger apartment.

They made a list of things the baby would need, which grew so long that it became a running joke.

They even started attending prenatal workshops.

In between all the madness, Arnab worked harder than ever.

He wanted to build a world safe enough, kind enough, **warm enough** for the little life now blooming inside Rhea.

Their Last Unforgettable Night

One night, about two months before the due date, they drove up to the hills outside Palo Alto to watch the meteor showers.

They lay side-by-side on the hood of their old Toyota Camry—Arnab's Tesla having long been sold to cover part of the new expenses—and counted falling stars.

"I hope the baby has your brain," Rhea said, tracing invisible constellations with her fingers.

"And your stubbornness," Arnab said, bumping her shoulder.

She laughed.

Then she grew quiet.

"What if we mess up?" she asked, barely a whisper.

Arnab turned to face her.

"Then we'll love harder."

One Last Dream

That night, as Rhea drifted off to sleep in the car, her head on his shoulder, Arnab looked up at the ink-black sky and made a silent vow:

No matter what happens, I'll keep this world beautiful for you. For both of you.

He didn't know then that the universe, with all its cruel brilliance, had other plans.

But in that moment, under a sky falling with stars, they had everything.

Absolutely everything.

Part 4 of 5 – The Collapse

The night had been bathed in celebration.

Inside the grand ballroom of the Westin Palo Alto, Arnab Chatterjee was toasted like a champion.
He had climbed to the top—**Head of AI Strategy** at NextGenCorp.

Rhea had shone even brighter—her pregnancy glowing on her beautiful face, her laughter ringing across the crowd as their friends clapped and cheered.

It was supposed to be the beginning of their forever.

It became the end of everything.

The Departure from the Party

They left the ballroom late, arms full of congratulatory flowers and baby gifts.

The night air outside was crisp, laced with jasmine and city lights.

Rhea leaned against his shoulder as they reached their car, tired but incandescent with happiness.

Arnab squeezed her hand.

"We made it," he whispered.

She smiled. "We did."

The Crash

The intersection came too fast.

The drunk SUV driver barrelled through a red light at 70 miles an hour.

Arnab barely had time to shield Rhea with his arm.

The crash shattered glass, dreams, and futures all at once.

The Hospital

Arnab woke up two days later in Stanford Medical Centre, bandaged and broken.

His ribs fractured, his shoulder dislocated, minor head trauma.

But none of it mattered.

Because when he asked for Rhea, the nurse hesitated.

When the doctor came, his voice was too soft.

"I'm sorry. Neither she nor the baby made it."

Time stopped.

The world bent inward like a burning photograph.

Arnab cried once, into his pillow, when no one was watching.

And then, a deadness crept into him.

Partial Recovery, but No Healing

Days passed in a fog of morphine and muttered condolences.

Friends visited. Cards piled up.
He responded to none.

Shaun, his reporting boss, called once:

"Take it easy, Arnab. We'll sort things out later."

Later never came.

The Ultimate Betrayal

When Arnab was finally discharged, walking with a limp and a scar on his forehead, he opened his company email out of habit.

At first, nothing seemed amiss.

Then—an HR announcement in the system.

A promotion.

Hari Sharma — the very man Arnab had recommended for termination six months earlier for incompetence—**was now the new Head of AI Strategy**.

Arnab read it three times.

Hari. His subordinate. His failure.

The man who had smiled during Arnab's party, who had clapped loudly when Arnab received his promotion award.

The man who now sat in his chair.

What Stung the Most

There had been no formal termination letter.

No meeting.

No severance negotiation.

Just… silence.

As if Arnab had ceased to exist.

As if grief had made him invisible.

Disposable.

The Breaking Point

He closed the laptop with a calmness he didn't recognize.

Packed a suitcase without thinking.

Rhea's pregnancy scan photos.
Their wedding bands.
The origami crane she had left on his laptop the night he proposed.

He left everything else.

Furniture. Job offers. Dignity.

They could have it.

He didn't belong here anymore.

Buying the Ticket

At 3:12 AM, at a sleepless, faceless hotel near SFO Airport, Arnab booked a one-way ticket on Air India.

San Francisco ➔ Kolkata.

No return date.

He didn't inform his friends.

Didn't write goodbye emails.

He simply folded his life into a carry-on bag and turned his back on a country that had celebrated his ascent and abandoned him at his fall.

The Final Look Back

From the glass wall of the departure terminal, he watched the Bay Area skyline one last time.

It looked distant.

Impersonal.

A mirage.

As the boarding call echoed, he touched the inside pocket of his jacket, feeling Rhea's photo resting against his heart.

He whispered:

"I'll find you in the place where roots grow deep."

And stepped onto the flight home.

Into the unknown.

Into Ashapur.

Part 5 of 5 – The Promise of Return

The low hum of the aircraft filled the cabin like a lullaby sung by tired angels.

Outside the window, there was nothing but endless blackness, punctuated by the occasional glimmer of city lights far below.

Arnab Chatterjee sat in **Seat 23A**, his tray table down, his half-drunk cup of water untouched. He had drifted in and out of uneasy sleep since takeoff, his body still aching from old injuries, but it wasn't the physical pain that kept waking him.

It was the silence.

The silence where Rhea's voice used to live.

Half-Dreams and Ghosts

Somewhere over the Atlantic, as the plane rocked gently, Arnab dreamed.

He dreamed of a hospital corridor endless and white.
Of Rhea standing at the far end, barefoot, laughing, waving for him to catch up.
Of tiny footprints—too small for adult feet—glowing along the floor.

He tried to run to her.

But the harder he ran, the further away she became.

He called her name.

And woke up gasping.

The Reality of the Flight

The cabin lights had dimmed to blue.

Most passengers were asleep, sprawled ungracefully across rows or curled against windows.

Arnab sat upright, staring at nothing, the seatbelt sign blinking faintly above.

The stewardess offered him another glass of water.

He declined with a small shake of the head.

He wasn't thirsty.

He was homesick.

Not for America.

Not even just for Ashapur.

For a version of himself that hadn't been stripped bare by ambition, by loss, by betrayal.

The Weight of His Memories

He touched the inside pocket of his jacket.

Inside, Rhea's ultrasound printout.

The last tangible proof of a future that would never be.

His fingers lingered over the creased edge.

He imagined what she would have said if she had been here.

"You're not broken, Arnab. You're just… beginning again."

Home, but Not the Same

He wasn't going back a hero.

Not the shining NRI son.

Not the Silicon Valley success story.

He was returning a man hollowed out, carrying only memories and an invisible grave inside him.

Would his parents see it?

Would they know?

Would Ashapur recognize the boy it once sent away, now returning as a man with a thousand cracks stitched into his soul?

He didn't know.

All he knew was that he had no choice.

Because **sometimes when the map burns**, you don't find your way by following roads.

You follow **roots**.

The Captain's Announcement

Somewhere between the time zones, the captain's voice crackled over the intercom.

"Ladies and gentlemen, we will be beginning our descent shortly. Please ensure your seatbacks are upright and tray tables secured. Welcome to Netaji Subhas Chandra Bose International Airport, Kolkata."

The words struck Arnab harder than expected.

Home.

He had made it.

He had survived.

A Small, Silent Promise

As the plane dipped lower into the warm embrace of Indian air, Arnab closed his eyes and made a vow:

He would find meaning again.

He would rebuild—not in glass towers, not with stock options, not with PR awards.

But with **people**.

With **roots**.

With whatever pieces of himself remained.

For Rhea.

For the child they never met.

For the boy who once believed letters could change lives.

The Landing

The plane shuddered as wheels kissed runway.

Passengers stirred, gathered belongings, prepared to rush back into the lives they had left behind.

Arnab remained seated for a moment longer.

Breathing.

Centering.

Letting the smell of damp earth, dust, and distant fires welcome him back.

Only when most of the cabin had emptied did he finally rise, adjust his crumpled jacket, and step into the aisle.

No fanfare.

No applause.

Just gravity reclaiming him.

And a future yet unwritten.

Chapter 5: Shadows of Paper, Sparks of Code

Part 1 of 5 – Resumes and Rejections

Ashapur woke up early.

The roosters didn't need alarms. The cows didn't wait for clocks. And the post office, with its red paint and rusted hinges, stirred like an old man stretching before his morning walk.

Arnab, however, stayed in bed.

The **sunlight slipped through the bamboo blinds**, dappled across his face, and still he lay there—awake, motionless, staring at the ceiling fan. It spun like time—circular, predictable, maddeningly slow.

In his hand, he held his **phone**. Not for scrolling social media or reading news.

But waiting.

Waiting for an email. A ping. A callback. Anything.

He had sent **forty-seven applications** in the last two weeks.

To unicorn startups. To research labs. To MNCs headquartered in Bangalore, Hyderabad, Pune, even Gurgaon—cities he barely remembered navigating anymore.

Some companies didn't reply.

Others said, "You're overqualified."

One offered a role half his last salary—with no relocation allowance and a mandatory six-day week.

Another ghosted him after two rounds of interviews.

And the rest?

Silence.

The Man in the Mirror

He sat up and looked at the mirror above the cupboard.

Not the sleek, smart-glass mirror from his California apartment. This one was **slightly oxidized at the edges**, with a crack near the top right corner. It made his face look… tired.

He hadn't shaved in a few days. His jawline, once sharp, was now unkempt. His eyes, once confident, had shadows beneath them.

He tried to remind himself of who he was.

Arnab Chatterjee.

Former Head of AI Engineering, Next GenCorp, Palo Alto.

Featured in TechCrunch once. Guest lecturer at Stanford. Panellist at multiple deep learning forums.

And yet…

Here he was.

Jobless.

In Ashapur.

Sending cold emails on patchy mobile data, using a resume that now felt like a myth.

The Silence of Ambition

He had rewritten his CV six times already. Added Indian keywords. Removed jargon. Switched PDF formats. Changed formatting from bold minimalist to blocky traditional.

Still, nothing worked.

He pinged three college seniors on LinkedIn—people he had helped back in the day. No response.

Even a Stanford classmate he once gave code to didn't reply.

He wasn't bitter. Just… confused.

Was he too specific? Too expensive? Too… foreign for a local role?

He stared at the screen of his old ThinkPad, now working like a tired horse.

No new emails.

No messages.

No signs.

Just his last draft:

Arnab Chatterjee
Artificial Intelligence | Systems Automation | Predictive Modelling
Ex-Head of AI, Next GenCorp | 12+ years in enterprise AI & scalable ML platforms

And yet, now, no one wanted to even speak to him.

Seema Devi Notices Everything

"You didn't eat again," his mother said from the doorway, holding a steel plate.

"I'm not hungry."

"You say that every day."

He sighed. "I'll eat later, Ma."

She didn't press.

Instead, she placed the plate—rice, dal, mashed potato with mustard oil—on the bedside table and sat at the edge of the bed.

"You used to jump for this as a boy. Remember?"

He nodded. "And you used to add extra salt."

"You liked that."

He smiled faintly.

She didn't ask about the job hunt. She never did. But her eyes did.

After a pause, she stood.

"Your Baba said he's going to the post office early today. It's pension day."

Arnab kept silent.

Then she said, softly, almost as if offering a distraction, "He said… maybe you could go with him?"

Arnab looked up.

"To the post office?"

She nodded. "Just to see. Or help. Or breathe a little different air."

Gourango's Offer

Later that evening, as they sat in the courtyard, Gourango finally spoke.

"Not everyone who has a degree works in a shiny building."

Arnab didn't respond.

"You're not made for doing nothing, Arnab. You'll fall sick like that."

"I'm trying, Baba. I really am."

"I know," he said gently. "But till you find your place again, why don't you come with me in the mornings? Just see what we do. Spend time."

Arnab considered it.

He had nothing else scheduled.

The walls of his room were closing in.

And his father's eyes held something he hadn't seen in years—**an invitation, not an expectation**.

"Okay," he said finally. "I'll come."

The Walk to the Post Office

The next morning, at 6:55 AM, Arnab tied his shoelaces and followed his father out of the gate.

The village was already awake.

Women washed clothes by the pond.

Children chased each other down the red path, schoolbags bouncing behind them.

The tea stall had smoke curling from its chimney.

And as they walked, people greeted his father with nods and folded hands.

"Postmaster Babu!"

"Namaskar, Gourango Da!"

"Is this your son? The one from America?"

Arnab smiled. Answered politely. But kept his eyes on the road.

They reached the post office in five minutes.

A small building, faded red, moss clinging to the bottom. A wooden board above the entrance read:

INDIA POST – ASHAPUR BRANCH
"Service before self"

Arnab stared at the board.

He'd read that line a hundred times as a child.

But now, as a grown man, it hit different.

Inside the Office

The inside smelled like **paper, ink, and dust**.

A fan rotated slowly overhead. Three desks. One old PC on a corner table, screen blinking like it couldn't decide whether to live or die.

A man in his fifties typed loudly on a keyboard. Another sat near a stack of ledger books. A woman near the back counter arranged parcels.

They looked up, nodded at Arnab.

"Sir, welcome," one said. "We've heard so much."

Gourango introduced them: "This is Arnab. My son. He'll be here for a while."

Arnab walked around slowly.

The filing cabinets were rusted. A stack of envelopes leaned against the wall like a paper landslide. There were files—*physical files*—dating back a decade.

The **one computer** was running on **Windows XP**. It took three minutes to open a folder. Internet: on and off.

And no one complained.

Because this was normal.

This was how India worked.

Reality Sinks In

Arnab sat on a stool, observing quietly.

People queued outside.

Each had a passbook, a photo ID, a request written on paper.

Nothing was digital. Nothing was quick.

A man had come for a pension update.

A young girl had come to open a Sukanya Samriddhi account.

A postman returned with torn envelopes, one wet from the rain.

Arnab turned to his father.

"How do you find anything in here?"

His father smiled.

"I have an index."

He pulled out a **large handwritten ledger**, pages numbered and tabbed with thread markers. Names. Docket numbers. Notes in blue ink.

"This is faster than the computer sometimes," he said.

Arnab stared in disbelief.

In Silicon Valley, databases fetched petabytes in milliseconds.

Here, his father fetched government pension records **with paper and memory**.

And still… got the job done.

Night Thoughts

That evening, Arnab lay in bed, eyes open.

The room was quiet.

But his mind wasn't.

He had seen a world that ran **without Wi-Fi**.

He had seen a system that survived not through innovation, but **through the sheer will of the people running it**.

And he didn't know whether to feel frustrated or… inspired.

His phone buzzed.

A recruiter had replied.

"Thank you, Mr. Chatterjee. While your profile is impressive, we're currently looking for a more budget-aligned candidate. We wish you success in your search."

Arnab closed the email.

And whispered to himself:

"Tomorrow, I'll go again."

Not because he liked it.

But because he **needed to understand**.

Part 2 of 5 – Among Dust and Files

The next day, Arnab returned to the post office, this time by choice.

His father had already left early as usual—bag slung over one shoulder, freshly shaved, a cotton towel draped over his other. Arnab followed the same path at 8:15 AM, a little later, but no less determined.

The village was buzzing. A bullock cart creaked along the road, kids were shrieking in uniform, and a temple bell rang from the east side of Ashapur.

The early sunlight poured across the cracked brick pathway like golden paint, lighting up patches of green moss and puddles from last night's drizzle.

By the time he reached the building, the red post office door was wide open, and the familiar smell of paper and boiled tea hung heavy in the air.

Postmaster Babu's Office

Inside, everything was exactly as he remembered.

Except now, Arnab was seeing it **with eyes trained on efficiency**.

The layout of the office was a nightmare for productivity. Three workstations scattered with papers. Cabinets leaning to one side like drunk guards. Fans that functioned with a whine, not a breeze.

There were *no labels*. No indexes on cabinets. No CCTV. No backup generator. The only power backup was a massive **lead-acid battery** in the corner that hummed like it resented being alive.

The lone PC had a CRT monitor—white once, now yellowing—and its mouse still had a **ball inside**, not an optical sensor.

Arnab sighed.

The People Behind the Desks

The staff, however, weren't as archaic as the furniture.

There was **Krishna Da**, nearing retirement, who managed most of the day-to-day ledgers and parcels. Calm, polite, unreadable.

Manoj, a younger clerk who typed rapidly and took pride in remembering pincode directories by heart.

Kiranbala Di, the only woman in the office, managed money orders, and knew every widow, disabled, and pensioner in the five nearby villages by name.

They worked like **clock hands in an antique watch**—ticking away, never breaking rhythm, despite every physical barrier around them.

Gourango sat at his usual desk—upright posture, square spectacles on nose, fountain pen in hand.

To the others, he wasn't just Postmaster Babu.

He was the **glue**.

The file whisperer. The codebreaker of bureaucracy. The man who made a hundred rupees reach a man in the jungle with just a ledger and a red stamp.

A Fish Out of Water

Arnab was given a stool.

"Sit anywhere," his father said.

He chose a spot near the filing cabinet and tried to stay out of the way.

But within minutes, instinct took over.

He started observing workflows.

Two women came for a recurring deposit closure. It took them **forty minutes** to get it done. Half the delay was in verifying handwritten passbooks and locating two linked forms from three years ago.

"Don't you have a central database for all this?" Arnab asked.

Krishna Da smiled. "We do. But it crashes if we open more than two screens."

"What?"

"Yes. And it's only operational when BSNL works, which it hasn't today."

Arnab looked at the router box—duct-taped and blinking weakly.

The Computer that Lived in Fear

The office's only computer was handled like a sacred object.

Manoj booted it once every hour to enter data in **Finacle**—India Post's legacy software.

"It takes 18 minutes to log in. If you make a mistake, you must logout and start again," he said, rolling his eyes. "And sometimes it freezes during sync."

The system had **no biometric verification**, no user profile segmentation, and **no automatic backup**.

"You keep everything on the desktop?"

"Yes. And on a USB. One that I keep tied to my drawer with a string."

Arnab stared.

This wasn't just outdated.

It was **fragile**.

It ran on faith, habit, and a constant prayer that the electricity wouldn't go out before "submit" was clicked.

A Day in Letters

Despite it all, people kept coming.

Farmers in sweat-stained shirts. School children bringing envelopes to be mailed to exam boards. Old men who came for the ritual of speaking to Gourango about pensions—even when they had nothing pending.

Arnab watched how his father treated each person.

With time. With dignity. With a kind of service that no app could replace.

An old widow brought two return envelopes and asked:

"Postmaster Babu, will you fill these? My hands shake now."

He took them. Inked the pen. Wrote slowly. Carefully.

When she left, Arnab whispered, "Why do you do all this when it's not even your job?"

Gourango didn't look up.

"It is my job," he said. "Service doesn't end at the counter."

Contradiction in Motion

Arnab was torn.

One part of him was repelled by the chaos—by the mismanagement, inefficiencies, the mountain of unindexed files, the tea-stained forms with illegible ink.

Another part of him was moved by the **humanity**.

This was a place where time bent to people, not the other way around. Where files were found not with search bars, but with memory and dedication. Where people weren't just entries in a CRM—they were known by their problems, their families, their rituals.

He watched as his father found a 1998 property document within 15 minutes—by cross-referencing **paper logs** and remembering that "the man had once brought raw turmeric as a gift."

How do you train a system to replicate that?

Evening Exhaustion

By 5:30 PM, Arnab was exhausted.

Not physically.

But **mentally**.

The rhythm of the office had overwhelmed him. Not with its speed, but its resistance to speed. It wasn't broken. It was simply **wired differently**.

And in all his years of building systems, algorithms, and neural nets—he had never designed for this kind of environment.

He stepped out.

The sunset had already begun bleeding orange across the rooftops.

The school bell in the distance rang once.

He leaned against the pillar and closed his eyes.

For the first time in days, he didn't think about job rejections or tech stack comparisons.

He thought about people.

And systems.

And how far apart they'd grown.

Part 3 of 5 – The Catalog and the Chaos

The next morning, Arnab arrived at the post office even earlier than his father.

He unlocked the front latch with the spare key Gourango had handed him the night before, surprised at the **weight of the door**—not physically, but symbolically. This building held more than ledgers and letters; it was a living memory box, ticking in bureaucratic rhythm.

He dusted off the chairs, wiped the table with an old rag from the cleaning shelf, then switched on the PC, half-hoping it wouldn't take **forever** to boot.

It still did.

The Index of Everything

When his father arrived, he carried a stack of hardbound **catalogue books** in his arm—aged, thread-bound registers with worn-out labels like "TDS-A/2005" and "Pending Enquiries – 2003 to 2012."

"What's that?" Arnab asked, sipping from the clay cup of morning tea.

"My system," Gourango replied. "Offline, but not unreliable."

He placed them on the table gently, as if laying down books of scripture.

Then he opened one.

Inside, columns ran neatly down the pages. No computer font. No printouts. Just decades of **handwritten records**.

Each entry had a reference number, a year, a subject, and—most importantly—a custom-coded symbol that indicated where the physical file was stored.

"See this?" Gourango said, pointing to a squiggle.

Arnab squinted. "Looks like a lowercase omega."

"That means it's under Shelf 4, third pile, behind the yellow folder marked 'Rejected Claims'. It's a symbol I created. We use twelve of them to map every corner of this office."

Arnab blinked.

"You mapped the entire post office… manually?"

Gourango smiled. "When you don't have software, you make your own logic."

Test of the System

Later that morning, a man arrived—thin, nervous, carrying a bag of documents tied with string.

He bowed respectfully.

"Sir, I need a copy of the 2004 land parcel verification form. It was submitted in my grandfather's name—Rajendranath Majhi. Someone at the Panchayat said it passed through this office for stamp registration."

Arnab stood aside as his father sprang into action.

He walked to the catalogue stack. Pulled out a book labelled **"Property and Stamp – Legacy"**. Flipped pages quickly but carefully. Ran his fingers down a column.

There it was.

RM/2004/LV-07

He read the accompanying symbol. Walked to the dusty shelf near the back. Removed two cloth-bound bundles. Pulled out a folder. Opened it.

Inside—yellowed paper. Stamp marks. Signatures.

Arnab's mouth fell open.

"You… you found it in less than five minutes."

Gourango chuckled.

"I told you. Offline. Not unreliable."

Arnab took the folder. Held it.

He had spent the last six years of his life working with real-time, distributed databases. Multi-tier architecture. Cloud environments with a fault tolerance of 99.99%.

Yet here he was, in Ashapur, watching a man with a **fountain pen and memory** outperform half the tools in Silicon Valley.

A System Built on Memory

Arnab was amazed.

But also… disturbed.

"What happens when you retire?" he asked his father later.

Gourango didn't answer immediately.

They were walking home in the late afternoon sun, the scent of frying puffed rice drifting from a stall nearby.

"The catalogue only works because you know it by heart."

"I've trained Krishna and Kiranbala. They know the basics."

"But the logic—the symbols, the depth of indexing… it's not sustainable."

Gourango shrugged.

"Nothing is. But we hold what we can, while we can."

Arnab felt a chill despite the heat.

This wasn't just a post office.

It was a fragile ecosystem, one person away from **collapse**.

Digital vs. Human Logic

That night, Arnab opened his laptop and began drafting a schema.

He mapped Gourango's system into tables.

File Code | Year | Subject | Symbol | Shelf Location

He created twelve symbol mappings. Then wrote a Python script that would allow basic searching using name and approximate year.

Within a few hours, he had a prototype.

It wasn't revolutionary. But it was something.

A bridge.

Between human memory and machine access.

He looked at it for a long time.

Then whispered, "Why didn't they build this already?"

The answer was obvious.

Because no one had **stood in Ashapur long enough** to notice the problem from inside.

A Crack in the Wall

Later that week, an issue arose.

An elderly woman came in tears.

Her pension had stopped.

Her name: Sulochona Devi.

Her records: Missing.

For three days, Kiranbala Di and Krishna Da tore through files. Nothing.

Arnab decided to try.

He asked her the year she registered—2012.

Then he opened the digital prototype, entered the surname "Devi", and narrowed the range to 2010–2013.

Four entries came up.

One had a handwritten note in the physical register—"See: Secondary Ledger – 2011 Corrections".

They found the ledger. Inside it, a scratched-out entry.

Turns out, her form had been filed under a **wrong pincode**—and was **never digitized**.

They corrected it.

Three days later, her pension resumed.

Sulochona touched Arnab's feet with trembling hands.

"You are a real postmaster now," she said, smiling through tears.

But… Not My Cup of Tea

Despite the success, Arnab remained restless.

The office had become **less foreign**—but not any more comfortable.

He admired his father's discipline.

Respected the staff's honesty.

Appreciated the humanity of the system.

But deep down, it wasn't his world.

He missed API calls and model evaluations.

He missed whiteboards covered with logic maps.

He missed digital logs that didn't smell of mildew and time.

He was helping.

But he wasn't *building*.

Not really.

Not the way he wanted to.

One More Rejection

That evening, he received another email:

"Dear Mr. Chatterjee,

Thank you for applying to AIPath Solutions. After reviewing your profile, we regret to inform you that while your qualifications are exceptional, your current experience level is misaligned with our current hiring needs…"

He stared at the screen.

Then at the ledger on the table beside him.

The silence felt louder that night.

Even the fan's whir didn't cut it.

Part 4 of 5 – Shadows of Legacy

The monsoon clouds had rolled in earlier than expected.

Ashapur's skies had gone from blue to bruised. By noon, a steady drizzle soaked the thatched rooftops, turned the earth into slush, and swelled the ponds until their banks were just suggestions.

Inside the post office, the air felt heavy—not just with moisture, but with years.

Arnab sat at a desk that hadn't been moved in decades, helping Krishna Da verify entries from a ledger. Raindrops struck the tin awning with metronomic urgency, while a gecko chirped from somewhere behind the racks of parcel forms.

He flipped through another register, careful not to tear the pages. His fingers, once trained to glide over keyboards, now bore small nicks from the brittle edges of old paper.

Gourango walked in from his lunch break, umbrella dripping.

"You've done more than most interns," he said, eyeing the aligned stack of verified entries Arnab had just finished logging.

"Still feels like I'm scraping moss off a banyan tree with a toothbrush," Arnab muttered.

Gourango chuckled. "Banyan trees live longer than software. Ask any priest."

Small Acts of Order

In the past week, Arnab had brought some **semblance of structure** to his temporary world.

He had categorized over 300 files into a basic Excel format.

He created **pre-printed slip templates** for common requests, cutting down the time spent writing the same line fifty times.

He even taught Manoj how to use simple keyboard shortcuts and install a lightweight PDF compressor so they could digitally store scanned letters in folders labelled by year.

The changes were subtle. No press coverage. No media buzz.

But people noticed.

Especially the villagers.

The Missing Parcel

One morning, an irate man stormed into the office. A tailor from the next block. His parcel of imported sewing machine needles had been marked "Delivered" on the national tracking website—but it hadn't reached him.

He was furious. Threatened to go to the police.

Arnab intervened.

He asked for the tracking ID.

Manoj checked Finacle—it showed the parcel signed off by someone named **Raju**. The problem? Raju was the neighbourhood's rickshaw driver, not the tailor.

Someone had signed on his behalf. But no one knew who.

Arnab asked Krishna Da, who remembered a **new substitute postman** delivering that day.

Together, they traced the record, scanned the ledger, and found a **mis-delivery**.

The parcel had gone to a different block.

Arnab cycled to that house himself, retrieved the unopened package, and returned it to the tailor.

The man folded his hands, ashamed of his earlier outburst.

"You're not like the usual officers," he said. "You listen."

That evening, when Arnab sat on the post office step in the fading sun, sipping tea, a child ran up and handed him a guava.

"Dadu said thank you."

Arnab smiled.

The Ghosts of Digital Dreams

But even in these small victories, he felt the shadow of something larger looming inside him.

This wasn't what he trained for.

This wasn't what the sleepless nights in Palo Alto were meant to become.

He missed innovation.

He missed brainstorming sessions that began with "What if…" and ended with breakthroughs that changed user behaviour across continents.

Here, "What if" got him blank stares.

What if we scanned all files?
Too expensive. No scanner.

What if we used QR codes?
Most villagers don't have smartphones.

What if we built an app for pension tracking?
Who will maintain it when you leave?

Every answer was an anchor.

And Arnab, despite all his empathy, still wanted to **fly**.

Talks with Seema

That night, as they finished dinner, Seema Devi sat beside him on the veranda, folding laundry.

"You've made this house feel like a home again," she said.

"I'm only half here, Ma," he replied, honest.

"I know. Your eyes still search beyond the trees."

He stayed quiet.

"You want to go back."

"I want to go forward," he said. "But I don't know where forward is anymore."

Seema looked at the sky, now clear, stars twinkling like breadcrumbs.

"Your father builds with what he has. You dream of what could be. Both are needed."

"His world runs on memory. Mine runs on servers."

"Then build a bridge. Just don't burn either side."

Arnab nodded.

He didn't have answers.

But her words gave him peace.

The Notebook

He had started carrying a notebook—a simple spiral-bound diary.

Inside, he sketched ideas.

A system that could classify physical files by barcode.

A mobile app with local language UI for rural banking alerts.

A low-cost document scanning system using Android phones with OCR optimization.

He even began conceptualizing a **hybrid system**—offline-first, battery-efficient, searchable via SMS commands for places without data coverage.

It was rough.

It was fragmented.

But it was hope.

Hope that he could combine his worlds.

And Then… the Letter Arrives

On a quiet Thursday evening, Arnab returned from the post office, dusty and drained.

He sat at his desk, booted his laptop, and connected to the 3G hotspot.

As he waited for the browser to load, he opened his inbox out of habit.

And then—he saw it.

Subject: Application Review – AI Head (Digitization Project)
From: Samanvay Systems

He clicked.

"Dear Mr. Chatterjee,

We are a technology partner for a Government of India initiative to digitize postal and rural administrative systems across Tier-3 towns and villages.

Your profile matches our requirement for an AI Head to design scalable models suited for infrastructure-light environments.

We invite you to a preliminary discussion this weekend.

We're especially excited about your roots in rural Bengal. That insight is rare."

— Team Samanvay

Arnab read it twice.

Then once more.

His hands trembled.

He stepped outside.

The stars looked the same.

The neem tree rustled softly.

But something had changed.

Inside him, a **spark** had returned.

A map was forming.

One that pointed both backward and forward.

One that didn't ask him to choose between soil and code.

He held the letter close to his chest.

And whispered—

"Maybe this is it."

Part 5 of 5 – Sparks of Code

The world felt different the next morning.

Nothing had actually changed—Ashapur still buzzed to its own rural rhythm. The chai stalls still hissed at dawn. The temple bell still rang at six. Cows still blocked the street. Power still blinked like an indecisive spirit.

But for Arnab, everything **had** changed.

That email wasn't just an opportunity—it was a sign.

For the first time in months, he felt **like himself**.

Not like a shadow of his former corporate identity. Not like the displaced NRI trying to adjust to power cuts and offline registers.

He felt like **the bridge he had been searching for**.

Samanvay Systems: The Proposal

The next day, he sat at his desk, his old ThinkPad humming away. Monsoon winds rattled the shutters, but he barely noticed. His fingers typed with precision.

He reviewed the attached project brief again:

"Samanvay Systems" was a mid-stage startup, part of a larger public-private partnership with India's Department of Posts and NITI Aayog.

They were looking to build a **pilot AI-based framework for rural digitization**. Their goals included:
Intelligent file classification and retrieval from physical archives.
Smart scheduling for mail and pension delivery.
Real-time error-checking in record management.
Low-bandwidth, offline-first architecture.
On-ground collaboration with rural post offices in **West Bengal, Jharkhand, and Odisha**.

Arnab's jaw clenched when he read the pilot zones.

Ashapur was in the map's projected roll-out radius.

He leaned back and stared at the spinning fan above him.

It was uncanny.

Fate-like.

First Call, First Spark

His Zoom call with the Samanvay Systems CTO, **Rishabh Sen**, was scheduled for Saturday morning.

Arnab dressed simply—white linen shirt, well-combed hair, and a calm face he hadn't seen in the mirror for months.

The video call crackled to life.

Rishabh was in his mid-thirties, bespectacled, sharp-eyed, speaking from a modest co-working space in Bangalore. Behind him, a whiteboard read: *"Don't Digitize What You Don't Understand."*

They exchanged pleasantries before diving in.

"I've read your proposal," Rishabh said. "Your stint at NextGenCorp speaks for itself. But what caught my eye was your recent location."

"Ashapur," Arnab confirmed. "It's where I was born. I've been helping my father—he runs the post office here."

Rishabh raised an eyebrow.

"You've been inside a rural branch?"

"Every day for three weeks."

"You know their workflows?"

"I helped resolve a missing pension. Helped digitize their file catalogue manually. Wrote scripts to trace errant entries."

Rishabh smiled slowly.

"You're overqualified, but also… the most context-aware person we've met."

He continued, "This isn't glamorous work. You'll travel to villages. Get your hands dirty. It's not about building a product, but changing a system that refuses to change."

"I don't want glamour," Arnab said. "I want impact."

There was a pause.

Then Rishabh said:

"Welcome aboard, Arnab. We'd be lucky to have you."

Returning to the Post Office—One Last Time

Arnab didn't tell his parents immediately.

He wanted one last day at the post office—not as a visitor, but as a witness.

The building greeted him like always, creaking with habit and heat.

He helped a woman fill a life certificate.

Assisted Manoj with a power reboot.

Scanned three more documents and stored them in his local archive.

Even helped a child write the address on an envelope to Kolkata University.

Then, around noon, he quietly pulled Gourango aside.

"Baba, I have something to tell you."

The Conversation

They sat in the back room—the one where older files were stacked like history books no one read anymore.

"I got a job offer," Arnab began.

Gourango didn't react immediately.

"With a startup in Bangalore. But the work is here."

"Here?"

"In villages. In post offices like this. The government's rolling out a rural digitization program. I'll be building the framework."

His father exhaled slowly.

"That's good."

"I'll have to travel. Work in the field. Some of it will be messy. But I'll get to… reimagine this. Make sure what you built doesn't get erased, but improved."

Gourango looked at him—eyes unreadable, lips pursed.

"You're going back to your world," he said finally.

"I thought I'd left it. But maybe I just needed a reason to bring it here."

Silence.

Then, softly:

"I never wanted you to be like me, Arnab."

Arnab frowned. "But you are—"

"I wanted you to be better," his father finished. "And this… maybe this is it."

Seema's Reaction

When Seema heard the news, she didn't react with cheers.

She just hugged him.

Held him tightly.

Then said:

"Just one thing. Don't vanish again."

“I won’t, Ma.”

“You can digitize the country. But don’t lose the people.”

“I’ve learned that now.”

She smiled, wiped a tear, and went back to frying fritters.

Because that’s what mothers did. They held you in their arms and then returned to the kitchen as if the world hadn’t just shifted on its axis.

Closing Scenes

That night, Arnab sat on the terrace under the stars.

Notebook in hand.

He sketched new versions of his earlier ideas.

Offline-first QR file tags.
Field-ready OCR kits for dusty documents.
Voice-to-text AI models for old clerks uncomfortable with keyboards.
AI workflow assistants trained on actual government formats.

He made a list of pilot branches to visit.

At the top: **Ashapur**.

He heard a rustling noise and turned.

His father was standing near the doorway.

“You’ll need this,” Gourango said, handing him something.

Arnab looked down.

It was a **red rubber stamp**—the one used to seal registered letters.

Faded, cracked, but still usable.

“Why?”

His father shrugged. “Every revolution begins with a seal.”

They both laughed.

And in that laughter, decades of silence melted.

Final Reflections

As the rain began again—soft, rhythmic, alive—Arnab looked out across the village, his home, his roots. He knew the road ahead would not be easy. The bureaucracy would fight. The systems would resist. The people would hesitate.

But he also knew:

This time, he wasn't running away.

He was stepping into the storm.

With code in one hand, and conviction in the other.

Chapter 6: Shadows of Deception

Part 1 of 5 – The Call That Almost Broke Them

The winter mornings in Ashapur had a way of creeping up quietly.

Mist clung to the fields like thin muslin draped over a dreaming world.
Cows stood in silent clusters, their breath steaming the cold air.
Children shuffled along muddy lanes with oversized schoolbags, their laughter muffled by woollen scarves.

Inside the old Chatterjee house, **Gourango** sat at the small wooden dining table, sipping his first cup of sweet black tea. The transistor radio crackled in the background with grainy announcements about wheat prices and district weather forecasts.

Arnab sat opposite him, scrolling through job listings on his aging laptop, battling the sluggish Wi-Fi that seemed to treat each webpage as a personal favour.

Life had settled into a **quiet, cautious rhythm**.

Until the phone rang.

The Scam Call

Gourango answered, his brow furrowed.

"Hallo? Ke bolchen?" ("Hello? Who's speaking?")

There was a pause, then a smooth voice in accented Bengali.

"Postmaster Babu! Boro khushi'r khobor! Congratulations! You have won the Government Digital Lottery! A car and a cash prize of five lakh rupees!"

Arnab looked up sharply.

Gourango's face brightened, confused but intrigued.

"Government lottery?" he repeated.

"Yes, sir! Your service to the nation has been recognized! You simply need to pay a small 'registration verification' fee to claim your reward. We will send a secure UPI QR code link. Please act within one hour, or you will forfeit this historic gift!"

Arnab was already on his feet.

He could hear the slick sales pitch bleeding through the speaker.

"Baba, hang up," Arnab said firmly.

Gourango waved him off. "Let me hear! Maybe it's real! They're speaking so nicely!"

The Intervention

Arnab grabbed the receiver gently but firmly.

He pressed the "End Call" button.

"Baba, that's a scam."

Gourango looked indignant. "How can you say? He knew my title! He said Government!"

Arnab knelt down beside him, heart pounding from anger and fear.

"Exactly, Baba. That's how they work. They target respected people, use half-truths, and rush you into action. No real government office will ask for money before giving awards."

He opened his laptop, pulled up examples of phishing scams.

Pictures of similar fake lottery messages.
Fake logos.
Fake government seals.

"They prey on trust," Arnab said quietly. "That's their weapon."

Gourango's shoulders sagged.

Embarrassment flooded his face.

"I almost believed…"

"You're not alone," Arnab said gently. "They design it to make good people believe."

Realization Hits

Seema entered the room, wiping her hands on her sari.

She sensed the tension instantly.

Arnab explained the situation.

Her hands flew to her mouth.

"Hai bhogoban! What if he had sent money?" ("Oh God! What if he had sent money?")

Gourango said nothing.

He stared at the blank phone screen.

The man who had navigated endless bureaucratic mazes, who had balanced registers blindfolded, had been almost fooled.

By a stranger with a charming voice.

Arnab saw something shift in his father's eyes that day.

Not fear.

Shame.

And that broke Arnab's heart more than anything else.

The Decision

That night, Arnab made a decision.

He couldn't protect just his father.

He had to protect all of Ashapur.

Every retired pensioner.
Every tea stall owner.
Every housewife and farmer who still trusted a ringing phone as a harbinger of good news.

Part 2 of 5 – The Digital Awareness Campaign Begins

The next morning, **Arnab stood under the giant banyan tree** at the centre of Ashapur village, watching the slow gathering of people.

It wasn't an official meeting.

No government orders had been issued.

No big banners fluttered.

Just a simple word passed from mouth to mouth:

Old men in dhotis and faded jackets ambled over with hands tucked behind their backs.
Women balancing vegetable baskets paused on their way to the haat.
Young boys circled around on rusty bicycles.

There was a buzz in the air—half curiosity, half scepticism.

Setting the Stage

Arnab dragged a battered blackboard and a small amplifier-speaker setup to the base of the tree.

Beside him stood Dulal, carrying a backpack full of homemade flyers.

Rajesh helped connect the speaker to a portable battery.

No stage, no glamour.

Just urgency.

And hope.

Arnab cleared his throat and tapped the mic.

It squeaked painfully.

He winced and smiled sheepishly.

A ripple of chuckles moved through the crowd.

Good, he thought. *At least they're still willing to laugh.*

The Opening Speech

He began in Bengali, his voice steady but respectful:

"Apnara shobai amake chinte paren—kintu ajke, ami ekhane postmaster'er chele hisebe na, apnader ekjon sartho-rakkhok hisebe esechhi."
("You all know me as the Postmaster's son. But today, I stand here as your protector.")

He held up his father's ancient money order receipt book.

"This… is trust. For generations, this book kept your pensions, your savings, your hopes safe."

Murmurs of agreement.

"But now, times are changing. Scammers, fraudsters, and cyber-thieves are trying to break that trust—not with swords or guns, but with phones and fake promises."

He paused, letting it sink in.

Demonstration of a Scam

Arnab had prepared a live demonstration.

He pulled out his phone, played a recording of a fake lottery call, exactly like the one his father had received.

"Sir, apni ekta boro lottery jitiyachen! Kintu age kichhu fees dite hobe!"
("Sir, you have won a big lottery! But you must pay some fees first!")

The crowd stiffened.

Several older men shifted uncomfortably.

Women looked at each other knowingly.

"They sound real, don't they?" Arnab said.

"They know your name. Your title. They sound polite. They use government words."

He looked around.

"But they are **liars**."

Signs of a Scam

Arnab chalked out **Five Rules** on the blackboard:
No government agency asks for money to release awards.
No bank will ever call asking for passwords or OTPs.
Never scan QR codes sent by strangers.
Verify every call by visiting the nearest post office or bank physically.
If it sounds too good to be true—it probably is.

He pointed to each rule, making villagers repeat after him.

Some laughed nervously.

Some frowned thoughtfully.

But they **listened**.

And that was a start.

Real-Life Examples

Arnab shared stories:
A farmer from the next village losing ₹30,000 because he shared his ATM pin over a "verification call."
A retired headmaster tricked into paying a "processing fee" for a fake Provident Fund bonus.
A widow who lost her entire savings believing she had "won a government housing lottery."

The gasps from the audience were genuine.

For once, technology didn't seem magical.

It seemed dangerous.

And very, very real.

Resistance and Scepticism

Not everyone was convinced.

An old man named Pradip Da stood up, leaning heavily on a stick.

"Baba, we lived fine without mobiles and computers. Why do we need this evil? What has it brought except thieves and lies?"

Murmurs of agreement from some elders.

Arnab smiled respectfully.

He nodded.

"Kintu Pradip Kaku, amader kaler din ghure gechhe. Technology will not vanish. Ignorance will not protect us. Awareness will."

He pointed to a boy in the crowd—maybe 10 years old—playing with a cracked Android phone.

"Your grandson already lives in that world."

"The question is not whether the world changes."

"The question is—**will we let the world change us without teaching us how to protect ourselves?**"

Launching the Campaign

Arnab announced a new plan:

Weekly Digital Literacy Camps outside the Post Office.

Workshops for farmers on spotting fake loan calls.
Workshops for women on safe mobile payments.
Training for elders on basic smartphone safety.

Anyone could join.

No fees.

No complicated English.

Just practical protection.

Response

At first, hesitant applause.

Then stronger.

Rajesh started handing out printed flyers Dulal had photocopied at the district town.
Bullet points in bold Bengali.
Cartoon drawings showing scam scenarios.
Emergency numbers printed in big font.

The villagers crowded around, reading, discussing.

Arnab stood back, heart swelling with something he hadn't felt since Rhea smiled at him across a broken Tesla:

Purpose.

A Father's Warning

Later that evening, as Arnab packed up the speaker, Gourango came up to him.

He looked tired.

Older than usual.

"Bhalo bolish. Bujhi. Kintu ei digital'er jug to chor-der shohoje kore diyechhe."
("You spoke well. I understand. But this digital world has made things too easy for thieves.")

Arnab smiled sadly.

"Baba, even paper can be forged. In every generation, scams existed. Some were letter scams. Some were fake stamp scams. Now it's mobile calls."

He placed a hand gently on his father's shoulder.

"Blaming the system won't save us. **Learning** will."

Gourango didn't argue.

He simply nodded, very slightly, and walked home slowly, the mist swallowing him.

Part 3 of 5 – First Success and First Doubts

Two weeks after the awareness campaign launch, **Ashapur looked a little different.**

The evenings under the banyan tree were no longer just for gossip and tea.

They were learning spaces now.

Villagers gathered in loose circles around a blackboard where Arnab and his small team taught simple, powerful lessons:
How to recognize phishing links.
How to set strong mobile passwords.
How to spot a fake insurance offer.

The sessions were messy, noisy, and often hilarious — but they were **working**.

And for the first time since landing in Kolkata, **Arnab felt useful again.**

Small Victories

During one of the first sessions, a teenage boy ran up to Dulal, waving his phone excitedly.

"Dada! I got a call from someone saying my uncle was in hospital and needed money immediately! I remembered what Arnab Dada said and asked for proof. They hung up!"

The boy's grin was contagious.

The crowd cheered.

Arnab ruffled the boy's hair and smiled.

"One less scammer winning today."

Another day, Kiranbala Di, the local vegetable vendor, showed up carrying her battered keypad phone.

She had gotten a text saying she won a foreign lottery and needed to "verify" her bank details.

Thanks to Arnab's teachings, she had immediately deleted it and warned three neighbors.

"Bachye dilen, Baba," she said, folding her hands in a pranam.
("You saved us, son.")

The Growing Buzz

Word spread beyond Ashapur.

Nearby villages sent messengers asking if Arnab could hold workshops there too.

Even the district newspaper published a small article:

"Son Returns to Safeguard Village with Digital Literacy Drive"

A reporter even interviewed Gourango briefly, who, despite his reservations, said proudly:

"Yes, my boy is making people smarter."

For a moment, it felt like everything was finally turning a corner.

Underneath the Applause: Seeds of Doubt

But success often hides quieter fears.

And Ashapur, like any old village, held its fears tightly.

Some elders muttered at tea stalls:

"Too much computer knowledge will spoil the simple folk."

"Next thing you know, they'll close the Post Office too."

"Today he's teaching safety. Tomorrow he'll take our jobs."

They whispered that **Arnab**, for all his good heart, was still a man who came from a world of emails and machines, not mud roads and money orders.

Signs of Trouble

Rajesh mentioned it first one evening as they packed up after a workshop.

"Dada… some people are saying… maybe you're preparing us… because jobs will be cut."

Arnab turned sharply.

"What?"

Rajesh kicked a stone at his feet, embarrassed.

"You know… like those big cities… automation, computers… no need for clerks anymore."

Arnab felt a cold stone settle in his chest.

He had come here to heal, not to create fear.

A Difficult Conversation

That night, sitting with Dulal and Seema over tea, Arnab confessed:

"What if they're right to worry? What if by teaching them, I'm pulling the rug from under their own feet?"

Seema touched his hand gently.

"Knowledge never kills, Arnab. Fear does."

Dulal added, grinning crookedly:

"If we stay ignorant, they will scam us. If we learn, maybe we can save ourselves—and our jobs too."

Arnab stared into his tea cup, thinking.

The battle wasn't just against scams.

It was against fear of change.

Fear of becoming **obsolete**.

The very thing he had once believed he was protecting against in Silicon Valley — and had failed.

This time, he wouldn't fail.

He couldn't.

The Decision

He would continue the campaign.

But he would also start a second phase:
Teach new skills, not just safety.
Empower, not frighten.
Build bridges between old ways and new—not burn them.

He would plant seeds so deeply that even fear couldn't uproot them.

Ashapur would not be erased.

It would **evolve**.

With dignity.

With heart.

Part 4 of 5 – Storm Clouds Gather

Ashapur's winter mornings were growing colder, but the air inside the Chatterjee house was growing heavier.

The mistrust brewing in the village had crept into their home like a slow, stubborn mist.

At first, it was subtle.

A hesitation when Arnab passed the tea stall.

A tighter nod from the village tailor who used to joke about Arnab's boyhood.

Whispers behind broken walls.

And now—this silence at their dining table.

Rumours Taking Root

It wasn't just strangers anymore.

Even some familiar faces had started murmuring:

"Teaching them digital tricks… soon they'll replace us."

"A postmaster's son turned agent of change—and maybe destruction."

The irony was bitter.

The same hands Arnab had protected from digital scams now trembled at the thought that he might erase their livelihoods.

Clash Over Dinner

That evening, over plates of steaming dal and rice, the tension snapped.

Gourango set down his spoon with a thud.

He looked up at Arnab, his eyes stern, voice low but cutting.

"Bhalo kore shun Arnab—shobai tor prashongsha kortese. Kintu shune rakho, jodi tomar notun notun digital chinta diye eder jibon'e aaghat anish, ami tomar mukh dekhbo na."
("Listen carefully, Arnab—everyone is praising you now. But mark my words, if your modern ideas destroy their lives, I will not be able to face you again.")

Arnab looked up sharply, the words hitting harder than a slap.

"Baba, I'm trying to prepare them… not hurt them."

Gourango's laugh was short and humourless.

"Tui janish, Ajit Da'r chele kal bole gelo, je tumi amader shikhachho kibhabe jaa automation hobe pore. Ki sukh?"
("You know, Ajit Da's son told me yesterday that you are teaching everyone so that they can be replaced by machines later. What joy will that bring?")

Seema placed a calming hand on Gourango's arm, but he pulled away.

"Ei notun notun siksha diye, tui kiser aasha dekhachhis? Shobai jaane, finally amader jaiga thakbe na."
("With all this new education, what hope are you really offering? Everyone knows, in the end, there will be no place left for us.")

Arnab's Hurt

Arnab stood up, chair scraping loudly against the floor.

He struggled to find words.

Anger, sadness, and helplessness twisted inside him.

"Baba, I am not teaching them to replace anyone. I am trying to teach them to survive."

He pointed toward the darkness outside the open window.

"Change will come whether we want it or not. Better to face it with preparation than to be swept away like dust."

A Cold Silence

Gourango said nothing.

He picked up his glass of water, drank it slowly, and set it down with deliberate calmness.

The silence between father and son yawned wide.

Seema looked from one to the other, eyes glistening, as if trying to stitch the invisible crack with just her presence.

But that night, no words could bridge it.

Arnab turned and left the room without another word.

His footsteps echoed through the hallway.

The old walls seemed to shrink inwards.

A Storm Inside and Out

Outside, the clouds thickened.

Wind howled through the palm trees.

Dogs barked in the distance.

Inside the house, three figures sat apart, each haunted by their own ghosts:
Gourango, trapped by fear of a disappearing world.
Seema, praying silently for her family to heal.
Arnab, wondering whether he was building bridges—or just burning them in the wrong places.

The rain finally came, first as a whisper against the tiled roof, then heavier, relentless.

Ashapur, and the hearts inside it, were bracing for a storm far greater than the weather.

Part 5 of 5 – The Calm Before the Storm

The rain had stopped by morning, but the tension across Ashapur remained thick and unmoving, like the wet mist clinging to the mango groves.

Arnab spent the day silently refining his plans, words scratching on paper louder than any voice inside the house.

Seema tried to keep the household rhythm normal.

Gourango remained distant, speaking only when necessary, his eyes shuttered behind layers of pride and old wounds.

Tomorrow would decide everything.

The Evening Before

As twilight draped the village in gray and gold, Arnab found himself wandering.

Past the old banyan, past the quiet tea stalls.

He reached the edge of the temple pond, where the land dipped into a slight hollow.

And that's where he heard it.

The Baul's Song

An old Baul, wrapped in a faded saffron shawl, sat cross-legged by a cracked wall, strumming his battered ektara under a sputtering hurricane lamp.

His voice rose slow and heavy, weighted with centuries of heartbreak:

**"Gharer chabi porer haate…
Bondho ghorer duar…"**
*(The key to my home lies in someone else's hand…
While the door to my own home remains closed.)*

The words drifted into the misty air, each note cutting deeper than the last.

Arnab stopped in his tracks.

His heart clenched painfully.

It wasn't just a song.

It was **his truth**.

The Echo Inside

He felt it in his bones.

The key to his home — to his father's acceptance, to the villagers' trust —
no longer lay in his hands.

He was a **foreigner** in the land of his birth.
An outsider at the door of his own legacy.

Everything he loved seemed guarded now by suspicion, fear, and unspoken accusations.

The Baul's cracked voice trembled on:

"Bondho ghorer duar…"
(The door of the house remains closed…)

And Arnab realized:
Tomorrow, when he stepped up to speak, he wouldn't just be fighting to prove a point.

He would be **fighting for his right to belong again.**

The Final Moment

As the Baul sang into the falling dusk, Arnab stood still for a long while, notebook clenched against his chest.

Not as a shield.

But as a prayer.

He turned back toward the house, where the faint lamplight glowed against the damp courtyard walls.

Tomorrow awaited him like an unopened letter.

Whatever it brought—
he would not run.

He would knock.

He would wait.

And he would hope that somehow, someone inside would open the door again.

Chapter 7: The Cost of Change

Part 1 of 5 – Back to Work, But Not the Same

Ashapur Post Office looked exactly the same.

Its chipped red paint, crooked flagpole, and creaky swing door hadn't changed an inch in the last three decades. The only difference today was the man standing before it—Arnab Chatterjee—not as the postmaster's son, not as the quiet observer he had been for the past few weeks, but as **the face of a new future**.

He was back, but this time, **on the record**.

Clad in a crisp white shirt, laptop bag slung across one shoulder, and a government-authorized audit letter folded in his pocket, Arnab stepped through the gate with purpose.

And instantly, the air changed.

Inside, conversations paused.

Eyes darted up.

The rhythm of paper-passing, stamp-inking, and register-turning slowed—not quite in respect, but in unease.

"Sir" Instead of "Arnab Da"

"Namaskar, sir," Manoj muttered, nodding formally as he moved aside.

"Good morning, Arnab Babu," said Krishna Da, lips taut, hands stilling on the ledger.

Even Kiranbala Di, usually chatty, offered only a short glance before retreating to her side of the counter.

Arnab noticed it all. The sudden addition of "sir" in every greeting. The shift in tone. The way they stood straighter when he passed by, like students in front of a new headmaster.

They had all known him as **Postmaster Babu's boy**—the lanky kid who once hid under the sorting table during a thunderstorm, the engineering student who used to carry hot tea for the clerks on his holidays.

Now, he was a stranger.

A possible threat.

The Letter of Authority

At 9:00 AM, Arnab convened a short team briefing.

They gathered near the main desk, sceptical but obedient.

He took out the printed document from his satchel and unfolded it on the table.

"This is the official mandate from Samanvay Systems," he began, keeping his voice calm. "We're partnering with the Indian government to pilot a rural post office digitization model. Ashapur is one of the first branches selected for the program."

Silence.

"The objective," he continued, "is to study current workflows, identify pain points, and recommend system improvements to enhance speed, reliability, and transparency."

Still silence.

His father had not come in yet. Arnab was glad for the buffer.

"I'll be spending the next two weeks documenting operations, talking to staff, and observing internal systems. Please continue your duties as usual. I'm not here to interrupt work."

Krishna Da was the first to speak.

"You'll… write about what we do wrong?"

"I'll write about what can be improved," Arnab said diplomatically.

Manoj's jaw tightened.

"Improved usually means replaced."

Arnab didn't respond.

Because he wasn't sure if it was a lie.

The First Walkthrough

He began his survey with the **register room**—the same place where he had once marvelled at his father's handwritten catalogues.

Now, he saw it with different eyes.

Deadweight paper. Unindexed cabinets. Crumbling file covers held together with tape and prayer.

He logged the number of shelves, estimated document counts, and marked each for priority scanning.

From there, he moved to the **cash counter**, watching how passbooks were updated manually, signatures verified by eye, and inkpads re-inked with small cotton balls.

In the back room, he observed Kiranbala processing a money order with three different ledgers open at once.

"Can I ask how long this takes per entry?" he said.

"About twelve minutes, if there's no mistake."

"And if there is?"

"Start again."

He noted it down. Didn't comment.

She looked at him with quiet resentment.

Gourango Arrives

By the time his father entered the building—umbrella in hand, the morning fog clinging to his kurta like cotton mist—the mood had already changed.

Arnab looked up, involuntarily straightening.

Gourango said nothing. Just gave a brief nod.

He moved to his desk without a word.

Sat down. Opened his inkpot. Began flipping through yesterday's mail.

Arnab tried to speak after a few minutes. "I briefed the staff about the project."

"Good," Gourango said without looking up.

"I'll need to ask you some questions too—about historical processes."

"You can ask."

That was it.

No welcome.

No tension.

Just the **wall of professionalism** his father knew how to build perfectly.

Arnab stood there, suddenly unsure which side he was standing on.

The First Rumour

At lunch, the murmurs began.

Arnab overheard two locals at the tea stall.

"They say he's here to automate the whole place. Bring machines. No more postmen."

"Postmaster Babu's son? He won't do that."

"They said he came from America. What do you think people do there? They don't use people, they use buttons."

Arnab turned away.

He didn't want to hear more.

But he knew it would spread.

In villages, rumours travelled faster than telegrams.

A Letter with No Return Address

In the afternoon, a woman came in with an envelope addressed to her son in Delhi. She asked Arnab how much postage to affix.

He calculated it, helped her stick the stamp, and handed it back.

"You're the postmaster now?" she asked innocently.

"No, just visiting," Arnab replied.

She squinted. "I heard you're bringing computers. Will we need to go to town to get letters now?"

"No, Aunty. The letters will still come."

She didn't look convinced.

"Hmm. Things change too fast these days."

Dinner at Home

That night, the dinner table was quieter than usual.

Seema tried to keep the conversation going—asked about mosquito nets, the temple renovation, her new pickle recipe.

But neither of the men spoke much.

Arnab chewed in silence. So did Gourango.

Finally, Seema snapped.

"This table is not a graveyard," she said sharply. "Either speak or leave your food."

They both looked up.

"I don't know what's happening between you two," she said. "But don't forget, both of you live under the same roof and serve the same people."

Arnab set down his spoon.

"I'm just doing my work, Ma."

"So is he," she replied. "Don't mistake silence for acceptance."

Gourango stood.

"I'm done."

Arnab's Notes That Night

Back in his room, Arnab opened his laptop and began compiling the day's notes.

He wrote in clinical, factual terms:
Manual pension verification system prone to error.
Absence of file tracking leads to data inconsistency.
Single-user access point causes bottlenecks.
No formal training program for digital upskilling.

He didn't write:

The staff fears for their jobs.
My father won't look me in the eye.
I'm becoming what I once promised never to be.

Instead, he saved the document.

Typed one word in the title bar:

"RESTRUCTURE_AUDIT_Ashapur_v1"

And shut the lid.

The fan spun overhead.

And the silence returned.

Part 2 of 5 – Resistance in the Air

The tension didn't explode.

It thickened—slowly, invisibly—like steam trapped in a closed kitchen, curling into corners, fogging up the glass. You didn't notice it right away. You just began to breathe a little heavier. You looked around more cautiously. You said a little less.

That's what the Ashapur Post Office became in the days following Arnab's official audit start.

A place where suspicion settled in like dust.

Everything Measured, Nothing Spoken

Arnab arrived each morning earlier than anyone else.

He began measuring things—literally.

The distance between workstations. The time taken to locate specific files. The number of steps it took from counter to archive. The average delay in completing pension dispersals.

He timed everything.

Documented everything.

Asked questions—but didn't always explain why.

"Krishna Da, do you remember how many pensioners submitted re-verification forms in the last fiscal year?"

"About 180," Krishna Da replied. "Maybe a few more."

"Can you show me those files?"

They spent twenty-two minutes locating a box beneath an unlabelled shelf.

Arnab wrote it down.

That was it.

He didn't scold, didn't smile, didn't say "thank you."

Only: "I have what I need."

When Data Becomes a Threat

Manoj, who had once shared jokes with Arnab over cups of tea, now avoided eye contact. He double-checked every entry twice before handing over any forms.

One afternoon, he stopped mid-task and asked:

"Sir… will this data go to Delhi?"

Arnab looked up. "Eventually. Why?"

"No reason."

But there was a reason.

Word had spread.

They believed he was auditing them for termination.

Not improvements.

Not support.

But **removal**.

And Arnab, trying to stay objective, said nothing to change the narrative.

The Whispered Question

It was around noon when a young junior staffer named **Rajesh** came to Arnab quietly while he was reviewing the parcel registry.

He was no more than twenty-five. Had joined two years ago. Worked part-time as a delivery boy and helped with basic entries on off-days.

"Sir," he whispered, glancing over his shoulder, "can I ask something privately?"

Arnab nodded.

They stepped outside.

The heat was sharp. The smell of mud and burnt rubber drifted in the air.

"Will… will we be replaced?" Rajesh asked.

Arnab was caught off guard.

"Why do you think that?"

"I read online. AI removes people. It works faster. Doesn't fall sick. Doesn't ask for salary. If this office becomes machine-run, what will I do?"

Arnab didn't answer right away.

He could have reassured him.

He could have told him something comforting, vague, or diplomatic.

But instead, he said nothing.

Because **he didn't know yet** what the final report would say.

And the truth was: if the system deemed this workforce "non-essential," they might indeed be replaced.

Rajesh nodded, interpreting the silence his own way.

He walked back into the office without another word.

Father and Son, Now Colleagues

Later that day, Gourango and Arnab found themselves alone in the backroom, both reviewing separate registers.

The silence between them was heavier than usual.

"You think this system is a joke," Gourango said suddenly, without looking up.

Arnab froze.

"I never said that."

"You don't have to," his father replied. "You walk around with that laptop like it's a badge. You note things as if they're faults. You act like this place should be ashamed."

"I'm just doing what I've been assigned to do."

"I've run this place longer than you've lived. Not a single rupee has gone missing under my watch. Not one pensioner has walked away with a false promise."

"I know that."

"Do you?" Gourango finally looked up. "Because it doesn't feel like you do."

Arnab stared back.

"I'm not here to mock what you've built."

"Then why does it feel like you're preparing to tear it down?"

At Home, The Quiet Cracks

At dinner, Seema tried to bridge the silence with talk of nearby weddings and mango pickle batches.

Neither man responded much.

At one point, she sighed, took off her glasses, and said:

"You know what hurts more than disagreement? Distance."

Arnab looked at his father.

Gourango kept eating.

That night, Arnab didn't open his laptop.

He lay on his bed and stared at the ceiling.

Outside, a thunderstorm brewed.

Inside, he didn't know if he was becoming the **villain** everyone suspected…

Or if he had just forgotten how to be **human** in pursuit of logic.

A Public Confrontation

The next day, it happened.

A local villager—an elderly man named **Haradhan**, known for speaking his mind—came to withdraw money.

While waiting in line, he turned to Arnab and said, loudly enough for all to hear:

"Postmaster Babu raised a son who returned not to serve, but to replace!"

Murmurs rippled across the room.

Arnab froze.

"I remember when you were this high," the man continued, holding out his hand at knee level. "Your mother used to send sweets for the clerks. Your father would carry you on his cycle."

Now everyone was staring.

"And now? You carry a laptop and want to carry us out!"

Arnab said nothing.

The man shook his head, took his slip, and left.

Even silence, Arnab realized, can be **a kind of verdict**.

The Shifting Wind

By the end of the week, fewer jokes were shared.

Less tea was offered.

The post office had become **a waiting room for anxiety**.

People watched Arnab not with curiosity, but calculation.

They lowered their voices when he entered.

And though he still worked silently, objectively, professionally—his presence was a weight.

He had become what they feared.

A sign of the end.

And he still hadn't told anyone otherwise.

Part 3 of 5 – The Audit Dilemma

The file on Arnab's laptop was growing every day.

What started as a handful of notes had evolved into an extensive audit: page after page detailing inefficiencies, outdated infrastructure, risk areas, bottlenecks, unrecorded delays, and staff roles lacking digital readiness.

By the tenth day, the word "redundant" had appeared eight times in the draft.

And yet, he hadn't hit save on a final version.

Because something inside him hesitated—though not enough to stop writing.

Two Columns

He stared at the document long past midnight one night, the glow of the screen painting his face with cold white light.

Two columns stared back at him:
Current Role
Future Viability

Each name had a corresponding assessment.

Some names—like Krishna Da and Kiranbala Di—had been tagged "functionally duplicable."

Others—like Rajesh—were marked "retrainable, pending skill assessment."

He wasn't writing this to be cruel.

He was writing this because it's what he was **trained** to do.

Because in Palo Alto, this is how it was done.

You mapped, measured, optimized, streamlined.

People became roles. *Roles* became metrics. *Metrics* became decisions.

He hated it. But it was the only model he knew.

Rishabh's Voice in His Head

He remembered a call with **Rishabh Sen**, the CTO of Samanvay Systems, earlier that week.

"Arnab," Rishabh had said, "your empathy is an asset—but don't let it become your obstacle."

"These are real people, Rishabh."

"I know. But we're not here to coddle. We're here to modernize. If the system doesn't move forward, it dies."

Arnab said nothing.

"Digitization is a scalpel, not a balm. And you were brought in to cut."

He'd nodded then.

But he'd felt like he was being carved out too.

Gourango's Handwriting

That morning, Arnab walked into the office early, hoping for silence.

Instead, he found his father already there—seated at his desk, bent over a register, pen gliding like it had for 30 years.

Arnab stood silently at the door.

He watched the lines of his father's posture.

The stillness. The concentration.

The way he paused every few minutes to rub his fingers, cramped from arthritis, before writing again.

The man was cataloguing dead files. Cross-verifying old death certificates with pension cancellations.

By memory.

Arnab felt something crack open in his chest.

But he still said nothing.

The Confession He Never Makes

That night, Seema Devi sat beside him on the terrace.

The moon was thin, almost embarrassed to be out.

She sipped tea while Arnab fiddled with the corner of his notepad.

"He's angry, you know," she said gently. "Your Baba."

"I know."

"He thinks you're here to erase everything."

"I'm not."

"Then why haven't you said that?"

He looked up at her.

"I'm afraid I don't know how to say it… without sounding like a lie."

She didn't push.

But her silence wasn't empty. It was *louder* than his words.

The Report Deadline

The email came at noon the next day.

Subject: Project Milestone Reminder – Preliminary Audit Due
From: Rishabh Sen

"Looking forward to your full regional summary, Arnab. Ashapur's report is critical—we'll be using it to template our approach across the Eastern zone. Please send your final document by end of day Thursday."

The weight of that message was more than digital.

It landed on Arnab's chest like a stone.

He opened the file.

Scanned the document.

There it was—his truth in text.

A report that could strip jobs, remove roles, and erase legacy.

He hovered his finger over "Send."

But his hand refused.

The Dream

That night, Arnab had a dream.

He stood inside the post office.

But it was empty.

No shelves. No papers. No fans humming. No voices.

Just **machines**—silent, blinking, cold.

In the corner sat his father.

Alone. In his chair.

Stamp in hand.

But no documents to seal.

No people to serve.

Just… **space**.

Arnab reached out—but couldn't move.

Couldn't speak.

Could only watch as his father grew smaller and smaller, until even the chair disappeared.

Morning of Dread

He woke up drenched in sweat.

The rooster crowed.

The light outside was already creeping up the veranda walls.

And the deadline loomed like a guillotine.

He got dressed.

He walked to the post office.

Did his tasks.

Spoke to no one.

Every smile felt like guilt.

Every "sir" felt like a scar.

The Final Scene in Part 3

At 4:48 PM, he sat at the corner desk—away from everyone.

He opened his laptop.

Opened the file.

Made final tweaks.

His cursor hovered over the word:
"Suggested role consolidation – 3 positions (including clerk, delivery assistant, data entry)."

He did not delete it.

He saved the document.

And closed the lid.

The report was ready.

But no one in Ashapur knew what was in it.

Not even his father.

And as the fan creaked above him, Arnab thought:

Maybe they never will… until it's too late.

Arnab hadn't realized how heavy silence could be until he had to carry it through dinner.

It wasn't that the house was quiet—there was the soft clang of steel dishes, the distant hum of a generator from a neighbour's home, the rustle of leaves against the window shutters. But no one spoke.

Seema placed rice on his plate, poured dal with practiced ease, and kept her eyes on the food.

Gourango ate slowly, deliberately, as though chewing each grain was an act of meditation.

Arnab wanted to speak. He wanted to ask about the temple renovations, the new schoolteacher who had moved into the village, or even the leaking pipe behind the kitchen—but his throat remained locked.

Because beneath the silence, they all knew the truth:

The report was written.

And they feared what it might say.

Gourango's Withdrawal

The next morning, Gourango didn't wait for Arnab before heading to the post office.

No call. No glance back.

Arnab found out only when Seema pointed to the empty teacup on the windowsill.

"He left at six."

"Did he say why?"

"He didn't have to."

Arnab nodded.

But it wasn't just about the office anymore.

It was about trust.

About betrayal without confrontation.

About the slow burn of knowing your own son might be the harbinger of **your obsolescence.**

The Village Begins to Pull Back

People had stopped talking openly around Arnab.

At the tea stall, conversations died when he passed.

At the temple courtyard, whispers trailed behind him like dry leaves.

Even Dulal, once his anchor, had grown distant.

When Arnab spotted him near the pond and waved, Dulal merely nodded, eyes wary.

He had become a symbol now.

Not of hope.

But of transition.

And no one in Ashapur wanted **that kind** of transition.

Seema Breaks the Ice

That evening, as Arnab sat on the veranda reading the same page of a book for the past hour, Seema brought him a bowl of puffed rice and sat beside him.

She didn't speak for a while.

Then finally:

"You were always different."

Arnab turned to her.

"You asked questions the other children didn't. You wanted to know why the moon had phases, why letters took longer to arrive in monsoon, why the doctor always wrote in English even for villagers who couldn't read."

He smiled faintly. "You remember all that?"

"I remember everything," she said, voice soft. "That's what mothers do."

He didn't respond.

"You were born to ask big questions, Arnab. But sometimes, the biggest question is… **how to do the right thing without breaking the people you love.**"

Arnab looked down at his hands.

"I don't know what the right thing is anymore."

"Yes, you do," she said. "You just haven't had the courage to say it aloud."

The Public Gathering

Two days later, a **notice was pinned** outside the post office.

"Public Discussion: Upcoming Rural Infrastructure Transformation – Ashapur Pilot Report to be Presented."
Date: Friday
Time: 11:00 AM
Venue: Village Panchayat Ground

It was signed by Samanvay Systems.

And by **Arnab Chatterjee.**

By morning, the village was buzzing.

Post office clerks glanced at each other but said nothing.

Krishna Da looked grim.

Kiranbala folded her hands in prayer after morning tea.

Gourango didn't even come in to work that day.

The Night Before the Storm

That evening, Arnab walked home alone.

Even the sky looked uncertain—clouds drifting lazily, a wind that couldn't decide its direction.

Seema stood at the door when he arrived, towel in hand.

She didn't ask anything.

But when he went to bed, he saw **a file tucked under his pillow**.

It was one of his father's oldest catalogue books—handwritten, annotated, aged to sepia.

Inside it, a slip of paper:

"When everything around you becomes noise, listen to the rhythm you started with."
—Baba

Arnab closed the book.

And sat in the dark for a long time.

Dawn of Doubt

The next morning, he put on a plain blue shirt.

Not the white official one.

No ID badge. No clipboard.

Just his laptop.

And a notebook.

When he stepped out, the village road had a different energy—**anxious**, like something waiting to be broken or saved.

He walked past the old banyan tree.

Past the library he once dreamed of building.

Past Ranu Didi's tea stall, where she didn't greet him.

And on to the **Panchayat Ground**, where the crowd had already gathered.

The Stage is Set

Three plastic chairs on a wooden dais.

Two loudspeakers crackling with occasional static.

Rishabh was already there, along with a local government officer and a translator.

The villagers sat in rows—men in white vests, women in bright saris, children weaving between their legs.

At the very back, leaning against a neem tree, stood **Gourango**.

Dressed in a spotless kurta, arms folded, eyes sharp.

Arnab took his seat.

And opened his laptop.

The report was there.

The truth, the findings, the recommendations.

He would present them now.

And no one—**not even himself**—knew what would happen after that.

Part 5 of 5 – The Storm Before the Calm

The night before the presentation, **Arnab didn't sleep**.

The ceiling fan spun overhead in lazy circles, but it wasn't the heat keeping him up. It was the weight of **forty-five names**—people with lives, families, dreams—whose futures might be rewritten by the report he was about to present.

He sat at his desk, laptop closed, notebook open.

The final draft was complete.

All he had to do was show it.

All he had to do was press **Enter**.

But something inside him wouldn't rest.

The Storm in His Mind

He poured himself water. Took a walk on the veranda. Listened to the frogs croaking in rhythm with the distant temple bell.

But his mind wouldn't quiet.

What if I'm wrong?
What if this hurts more than it helps?
What if Baba never forgives me?

He found himself speaking aloud.

"They'll hate me before they understand me."

He turned to the shadows.

"And what if they never understand me at all?"

At some point before dawn, exhaustion pulled him under.

And in the folds of sleep, she appeared.

Rhea.

Standing barefoot on the red soil of Ashapur, her white dress stained with sunlight and breeze.

She smiled—soft, knowing.

"Why so serious, Arnab?"

"I'm scared," he whispered.

"Of what?"

"Of losing what's left of him."

She stepped closer.

"You never lost him. You only stopped believing that he'd come with you."

He didn't speak.

"You're not here to destroy," she said. "You're here to evolve. The bridge is always the hardest place to stand."

He nodded.

She touched his chest.

"You're still the best person I ever knew."

Then she faded.

And the birds began to sing.

The Morning: A Village on Edge

By 9:00 AM, **Ashapur was tense**.

The panchayat ground had been swept. Three plastic chairs were placed under a temporary shamiana. A white screen stood at the centre.

Two local police constables stood near the entrance, hands on batons, scanning the growing crowd. They weren't here for ceremony. They were here for **precaution**.

Word had spread of potential unrest.

That the postmaster's son had returned not to serve, but to sanction.

Villagers whispered, clustered, speculated.

Would the post office shut down?

Would jobs vanish?

Would the old ways die?

The Government Arrives

At 10:00 AM sharp, two white Ambassador cars rolled up.

From them emerged **officials** from the regional Postal Directorate and the district administration.

One wore dark glasses and carried a folder of prepared statements.

The other, a younger officer, looked visibly uncomfortable.

They were escorted to the front row.

A few photographers from local dailies had arrived too.

The crowd swelled past two hundred.

And yet, silence prevailed.

Arnab, the Speaker

Arnab stood behind the makeshift stage curtain, staring at his reflection in a cracked mirror someone had leaned against a pole.

His hands trembled.

He wiped his palms on his kurta.

"Just speak the truth," he whispered.

"But whose truth?" another voice inside him replied.

He gripped the edge of the table behind him.

Then, a moment of stillness.

A memory of Rhea's voice:
"You're still the best person I ever knew."

He exhaled.

And stepped into the light.

The Crowd Turns

He was greeted not with applause, but with silence.

Not with welcome, but with weight.

Eyes locked on him.

Some with betrayal.

Some with hope.

His mother sat in the second row, a prayer on her lips.

His father stood at the back, near the neem tree, unmoving.

In his cloth bag was a metal container.

Kerosene.

Just in case.

Setting the Stage for the Climax

Arnab took the mic.

Behind him, a white screen flickered with the first slide.

Ashapur Post Office – Audit and Digital Integration Report

His voice rang through the loudspeakers.

"Namaskar," he began. "I stand before you not just as the son of this village, but as a professional tasked with presenting a difficult truth."

The screen changed.

Charts. Delays. Workflows. Redundancy models.

Tension grew.

He continued.

"This project is meant to create a future-ready rural communication network. But to do that, we have to ask: what parts of our system still serve us, and what parts must evolve?"

A wave of murmurs swept the audience.

He flipped the next slide.

Redundant Roles – 45 Identified

Gasps, Cries, Whispers.

Seema closed her eyes.

The constables stepped forward slightly, alert.

The government officials exchanged glances.

And **Gourango opened his bag**.

The tin clanked softly.

The kerosene glimmered faintly under the tent.

Arnab saw it.

But didn't stop.

Not yet.

Chapter 8: The Bridge Between Worlds

Part 1 of 5 – The Match is Struck

Time froze.

The matchstick flared to life—orange, sharp, volatile—in the trembling hands of **Gourango Chatterjee**, as over two hundred villagers watched in stunned silence.

The sharp scent of kerosene saturated the humid air. Sweat glistened on foreheads. Children clung to their mothers. The officers from the district administration leaned forward in alarm. The two policemen near the perimeter broke formation, stepping in with urgency. Seema stood up, voice lost in her throat. Dulal shouted, "Postmaster Babu, no!"

But Gourango didn't move.

His eyes were not wild. They were resolute.

The flame in his hand wasn't just fire—it was **a lifetime of service**, a statement of protest, a cry for dignity from a man who had given everything to the very institution now being threatened by the son he once raised with trembling pride.

On Stage, Arnab Didn't Move Either

He stood behind the podium, the blue fabric trembling slightly with the breeze. His mouth had gone dry. The projector light made his face appear pale and ghost-like.

The match in his father's hand burned lower.

And in that second—just before chaos could erupt—**memories surged like a dam breaking**.

Flashback: A Boy, An Inkpot, A Sunday Afternoon

He was six. Sitting on his father's lap. Watching the swish of a fountain pen across brown paper envelopes.

"Always tilt the nib at this angle," Gourango had said, guiding the little hand. "Let the ink flow, don't force it."

Arnab had asked, "Why do we write letters when phones are faster?"

Gourango had smiled, pressing the seal down firmly.

"Because a letter is a piece of time. It reaches someone's hand with your soul on it."

Present: A Man Caught Between Fires

The flame in his father's hand trembled but held.

Arnab's breath quickened. His heart thudded against his ribs.

He could have screamed.

He could have rushed forward.

But something deeper than instinct held him still.

Instead, he spoke—his voice low, even.

"I haven't finished."

It wasn't a command.

It wasn't a plea.

It was a statement of truth.

Gourango's eyes flickered. The flame hovered inches from his sleeve.

"I haven't finished," Arnab repeated, louder now, into the mic. "The list of redundancies is not the end of this presentation. It is the **beginning**."

Gasps Rippled Through the Crowd

One of the constables stepped forward.

Seema clutched the railing in front of her. Her lips moved in silent prayer.

Even Rishabh, seated at the edge of the dais, looked at Arnab in alarm. This wasn't part of the approved script. This wasn't expected.

But Arnab had made a choice.

He wasn't going to be the destroyer.

He was going to be **the bridge**.

And he needed to walk across it now.

The Flame Faltered

Gourango blinked.

The match burned down to his knuckles. The pain was real—but it didn't compare to the storm in his chest.

His son was speaking—not just with data, but with conviction.

"I have seen the pain of this place," Arnab said, louder now. "I've seen how one register holds fifty years of memory. I've seen how you, Baba, can find a file from 1987 faster than a computer ever will."

He turned to the crowd.

"But I've also seen what happens when someone's pension is delayed three months because the internet goes out, or when a clerk retires and no one can read their notes."

Rhea's Voice Echoed in His Mind

"You are still the best person I ever knew."

He gripped the podium.

"I made this presentation to show what must change. But what I didn't tell you… what I waited until this moment to say… is what will remain."

He looked directly at his father.

"And that is **you**."

The Flame Goes Out

A gust of wind swept through the tent.

The match, finally burning down to its base, fizzled against Gourango's palm.

He dropped it.

It hit the ground without a sound.

But the Storm Was Not Over

Gourango didn't collapse.

He stood tall.

"You play with words well," he said, voice cold. "But sometimes, change is a thief. It wears noble clothes but steals without guilt."

Arnab nodded slowly.

"I know," he replied. "That's why I didn't come to steal. I came to transform—with you by my side."

He paused.

"And I will tell you **how**. But not yet."

He stepped back from the mic.

"My name is Arnab Chatterjee. I am the son of a man who built a kingdom of paper and trust. And tomorrow—if you will let me—I will show you how that kingdom can rise again… without losing a single brick."

Scene Ends in Breathless Silence

The mic was set down.

The screen turned dark.

The crowd stood still, as if the wind had left them.

Seema began to weep—not from fear now, but from sheer emotional exhaustion.

The constables relaxed.

The district official adjusted his glasses.

And slowly, ever so slowly…

Applause began.

Not loud.

Not rowdy.

But steady.

From the back.

From the edge.

From those who understood that they had just witnessed **a man walk the tightrope between love and revolution**—and not fall.

Part 2 of 5 – The Unveiling of a New Legacy

The tent settled into a stunned hush. Dust from the crowd's shuffling feet hung visibly in the slanted sunlight. Somewhere nearby, a baby cried briefly before being hushed. Even the birds in the peepal tree seemed to hold their songs.

On stage, **Arnab stood silently** for a moment longer, hands resting lightly on the podium.

Then, he stepped forward.

The projector screen behind him flickered back to life.

Slide 18 of 30
Proposal: Human-First Rural Digitization Framework – Phase I: Ashapur

---

Not a Layoff List—A Lifeline

"Let's make one thing clear," Arnab began, voice steady now, emboldened by the silence, "those 45 names on the screen—those aren't people to be discarded."

He paused.

"They're the foundation of something new."

The screen changed again.

This time, it showed **new role titles**, next to familiar names.
Krishna Das → Senior Workflow Officer – Record Transition Lead
Kiranbala Devi → Community Support & Digital Entry Specialist
Rajesh → Field Data Navigator & Postal Delivery Automation Tester
Gourango Chatterjee → Legacy Systems Mentor & Cultural Knowledge Advisor

Gasps rippled through the crowd.

Gourango, still standing at the back, blinked.

His name?

His new designation?

He looked at the screen, then at his son, as if trying to decide whether to believe what he was seeing.

Not Replacement—Elevation

Arnab's voice became warmer, fuller.

"I spent weeks watching this place—watching my father navigate paper chaos with memory sharper than any processor."

He stepped down from the stage and walked toward the first row.

"You can't teach that. But you can **preserve it**."

He turned to face the villagers.

"You thought I came to erase your jobs. I didn't. I came to **rewrite them**, so they could survive in a world that is changing—whether we like it or not."

Slide after slide appeared.

Mock-ups of:
Training modules in Bengali and Odia
Voice-assisted data entry software
Offline-first systems with SMS-based commands
AI algorithms built to mirror Ashapur's file retrieval logic

Turning Catalogues into Culture

Then, the most powerful slide of all:

"The Ashapur Archive Project – Preserving the Past to Inform the Future."

Arnab explained:

"We will scan every catalogue. Not to discard the paper, but to build a searchable, teachable, **living archive** of how India's oldest knowledge systems functioned."

He pointed to a photograph of his father's handwritten index book.

"That is not outdated. That is **genius**."

A few claps rose from the left side of the crowd.

He continued, "Veterans like my father will mentor young trainees to help them understand not just data, but *context*—why records are written a certain way, how errors are traced, how trust is built over decades."

Reactions from the Ground

Seema was crying freely now, the kind of cry that only comes from watching your family nearly fall apart and then somehow **miraculously hold**.

Rajesh, sitting on the outer edge of the seating area, raised his hand hesitantly.

Arnab gestured to him.

"Sir… does this mean we will… still be needed?"

Arnab smiled.

"You're not just needed, Rajesh. You're **crucial**."

More applause followed. Genuine. Loud. Giddy.

Even Kiranbala Di, still holding her shawl, let out a soft, astonished laugh.

Gourango Steps Forward

But one person still hadn't moved.

Gourango.

Until now.

With steady steps, he walked toward the dais.

No kerosene. No fire.

Only a silence that parted the crowd as he passed.

He stopped in front of Arnab.

Looked into his son's eyes.

And after what felt like a lifetime, said:

"You rewrote the whole system… and kept us all inside it."

Arnab's voice broke.

"I had to."

Then, quietly—just for them to hear:

"Because you never threw me out of your world when I failed."

They embraced.

And the applause turned thunderous.

Part 3 of 5 – Father and Son Reconciled

The embrace between **Gourango and Arnab** wasn't loud or dramatic.

There were no grand declarations, no cinematic music.

It was just two men—father and son—standing on a makeshift dais beneath a monsoon sky, their arms around each other as the weight of **misunderstanding, pride, and years of distance** dissolved in silence.

In that single moment, more than a hundred villagers felt a surge in their throats.

Some wiped tears.

Others clapped again—this time slower, more rhythmically.

Like a **salute** to resilience.

Like the closing of a rift everyone had quietly feared would never heal.

"You Should've Told Me Sooner"

Gourango stepped back and looked at his son.

"You should've told me sooner."

Arnab nodded. "I should have."

"You made me think you were one of them."

"I did. For a while."

"But you were never one of them, were you?"

"I tried to be," Arnab said softly. "But I forgot where I came from."

An Apology Without Words

There was no need for "sorry."

Not in a place like Ashapur.

Here, wounds healed through **gesture**, not grammar.

The words didn't matter.

What mattered was that they now stood **on the same side** of the fight.

Seema Joins Them

Seema was the next to step forward.

The moment she saw her two men side by side, something inside her released.

She covered her mouth, then reached out to Arnab and hugged him tight.

Then she hugged Gourango, whispering something in his ear that made him nod and smile.

Rishabh, standing off to the side, whispered to the young postal officer beside him, "This… this is bigger than our pilot program."

The officer nodded. "This is history."

Words from the District Officer

One of the local government officials was invited on stage.

He adjusted the mic and began:

"Friends of Ashapur, I have attended many digitization launches. But I have never seen one with this kind of soul. Usually, we speak about systems and KPIs and efficiencies. Today, we have seen what it means to integrate not just processes—but people."

He turned to Arnab.

"You didn't modernize a building. You preserved a legacy."

More applause followed.

The constables in the back smiled and leaned their sticks against the wall. There was no unrest now—just **relief**.

The Official Declaration

The officer opened a sealed envelope and read aloud:

"By the authority of the District Administration and the Department of Posts,

we hereby declare **Ashapur Post Office** to be the official launch site of
the *Human-First Digitization Pilot Project – Phase One.*

Training, equipment, and onboarding shall begin within two weeks.

Legacy staff shall be retained and reassigned under the Adaptive Role Structure.

The cataloguing system of Mr. Gourango Chatterjee shall be digitized and archived
as a reference model for heritage-driven transformation."

Gasps.

Cheers.

Even the older clerks who hadn't smiled in weeks **stood up to clap.**

Rajesh Volunteers

Rajesh stepped forward nervously.

"I… I'd like to be the first trainee," he said, glancing at Arnab, then at the crowd. "I want to
learn. I want to stay. I want to… help."

Gourango clapped him on the back.

"Good boy," he said. "That's the spirit."

Dulal's Decision

Dulal, who had kept his distance all along, walked over and handed Arnab a folder.

Inside were diagrams, drawings, sketches of low-cost scanner setups and document holders.

"I made these the day after you scanned that old pension file. Didn't know if you'd stay long
enough to use them."

Arnab smiled, eyes glassy.

"Will you join us?"

"I'm not good with big offices," Dulal said.

"But you're good with building things," Arnab replied. "We need that."

Dulal nodded, wordlessly.

Preparing the Archives

That afternoon, something beautiful happened.

With the projector turned off and the official ceremony over, the villagers stayed back to watch the first **scanning of the legacy catalogues.**

Arnab, with gloves on, gently laid out the first of his father's ancient index books.

A scanner—hooked to a basic laptop and powered by solar backup—began its soft hum.

Page after page.

The story of a village.

The work of decades.

Digitized. Preserved. Respected.

Seema, Watching From Afar

Seema stood at the back of the room, hands folded, watching Arnab train Rajesh how to use the scanner while explaining the metadata structure.

Her son had returned.

Not just physically—but with **purpose.**

Part 4 of 5 – The Ashapur Declaration

Ashapur had never made headlines before.

It was a dot on the map, nestled between banana groves and railway tracks, known mostly for its honest postmaster and its evening tea stalls. But on that monsoon-soft afternoon, **history was made**—not because it changed the world, but because it proved the world **could** be changed without erasing where it came from.

Ashapur Declared Official Pilot Site

Two days after the presentation, a laminated sign was nailed beside the office door:

🏛 "Ashapur Post Office – Phase 1 Pilot for Human-First Rural Digitization"
Initiated by: Samanvay Systems in collaboration with the Department of Posts, Government of India

Local newspapers ran the story.

"Postmaster's Son Returns to Save, Not Replace."
"From Catalogs to Cloud: Ashapur Shows the Way."

A Bengali news channel came to film a segment. Their reporter—excited, umbrella tucked under her arm—interviewed villagers and captured Arnab scanning registers while his father looked on, arms crossed and proud.

Training Begins

By the end of the week, the post office had received:
Two laptops with extended battery life
A document scanner and barcode printer
Wi-Fi hotspot with offline sync functionality
Printed Bengali-language training manuals
Basic ID badges for new digital designations

Inside the newly cleaned "training room" (once a dusty storeroom), Arnab began with a chalkboard.

"Technology is not a replacement," he wrote. "It is an **amplifier** of good systems."

New Roles Take Shape

The old roles were not discarded—they were **reborn**.
Krishna Da became **Senior Digital Records Officer**, tasked with verifying all migrated data for fidelity.
Kiranbala was named **Community Access Lead**, managing pensioner transition support and bilingual helpdesks.
Rajesh assisted Arnab directly in setting up workflows and testing SMS-triggered reports.
Two retired clerks from nearby villages volunteered to act as cross-branch record interpreters.
Most beautifully, **Gourango Chatterjee** assumed his new title:
"Chief Knowledge Mentor – Ashapur Digitization Cell."

His first act?

Drawing a diagram—by hand—of how to find parcel records using mnemonic memory anchors. Arnab uploaded the scanned page to the central learning portal with the tag:
#legacylogics #AshapurMentor01

A Symbolic Ceremony

The district officer, Rishabh, and Arnab organized a small ceremony a week later.

Not for media.

Not for politics.

But for **symbolism**.

They placed the **first handwritten register**—a 1983 ledger with curled edges and red thread binding—into a glass-front cabinet labelled:

"The Ashapur Archive – Where Memory Meets Machine."

A digital copy was uploaded that very evening.

It was accessible across the pilot regions.

A ripple had started.

Schoolchildren Visit

A few days later, a group of schoolchildren arrived on a field visit.

Arnab smiled as they listened to Kiranbala explain the transition from passbooks to digital cards.

A boy raised his hand. "Did this office always have computers?"

"No," she smiled. "We used to sort everything by smell and memory."

Laughter.

Then awe.

Gourango showed them his coded symbols and told stories of letters that changed lives.

Arnab stood near the door and watched.

His dream was working.

But more importantly—**it belonged to everyone now.**

Dulal's Innovation

Dulal built a low-cost scanning frame using old cycle rims and wooden planks.

"Sometimes machines need jugaad too," he said, grinning.

Arnab uploaded the design on an open-source forum. It was downloaded **by five other pilot sites**.

One even messaged back:

"Never imagined a rural post office would give Silicon Valley a hack worth emulating."

Letters Begin Again

In the weeks that followed, the volume of actual letters increased.

Maybe it was nostalgia.

Maybe it was pride.

But villagers began to write again—to family, to officials, even to themselves.

One envelope caught Arnab's eye:

"To the Future Arnab – Please don't forget what this feels like."

He smiled, scanned it, and slipped it into a personal folder.

The Final Class

One evening, during a golden sunset, Gourango led his first full training class.

He stood with a piece of chalk, explaining file tree logic using mudra references from local folk dances.

Arnab leaned in the doorway and watched silently.

He didn't need to lead.

This was his father's moment.

From fire to foundation.

Part 5 of 5 – A New Dawn

Segment 1: The Morning That Felt Different

The morning sun poured across Ashapur like a new beginning. The soft orange haze filtered through the neem leaves and rooftops tiled with age and stories. Smoke curled lazily from clay ovens. Cows moved unhurriedly along muddy lanes. And the post office—once a symbol of resistance to change—now stood with its **glass-framed legacy catalogue**, its newly painted signboard, and a pride that **didn't fear progress anymore**.

The rhythm of the village had changed.

It wasn't just about new gadgets or roles.

It was a **change in heartbeat**.

In the tea stall outside the temple, Dulal wiped glasses with a rag and turned up the transistor volume.

"…and from the quiet village of Ashapur, a transformation not just in technology but in thinking," the announcer said. "Forbes India features local technocrat Arnab Chatterjee, whose design brought soul to systems…"

"Turn it up!" someone shouted.

People gathered—rickshaw-pullers, fruit sellers, the fishmonger with his cane basket.

The name "Arnab" wasn't just a name anymore.

It was **a mirror of what was possible**.

In the post office, Rajesh helped an elderly woman with her pension form, guiding her fingers on the new touchpad.

"No need to worry, Amma. Just press here. Yes—now the system knows you're here."

From the doorway, Kiranbala watched him, smiling faintly.

And outside, under a tree with one foot on a rusted cycle pedal, stood Arnab Chatterjee, **silent**, drinking all of it in.

The Forbes Feature and the Call from the Past

It was a little after 11 AM when Dulal rushed into the post office waving a crisp copy of the day's **Statesman**.

"Postmaster Babu! Arnab Da! Look—look at this!"

He unfolded the broadsheet with exaggerated care and spread it across the centre table like it was a national flag.

There, on **Page 3**, beneath the banner headline:

"The Man Who Digitized a Village Without Deleting Its Soul"

was a half-page article, and right in the middle—**Arnab's photograph**, taken during the ceremony when he scanned the first register with his father by his side.

Arnab's Reaction

Arnab stepped forward slowly, reading the first few lines in disbelief.

"From Palo Alto boardrooms to the clay lanes of Bengal's Ashapur, Arnab Chatterjee's journey is more than a tech comeback—it is an ode to the unsung legacy of India's postal past…"

He let out a breath he didn't realize he was holding.

Behind him, Kiranbala clapped softly. Manoj let out a grin. Even Krishna Da removed his glasses, wiped them with his handkerchief, and whispered, "Your mother must be glowing today."

Arnab didn't speak. But he nodded.

Because the truth was—**it still didn't feel real**.

A Buzzing Phone

At 1:14 PM, his phone rang.

Unknown number.

International code: **+1**.

His fingers stiffened around the device.

He knew that number format.

It came from a life he had buried deep under spreadsheets, airport layovers, and a coffin that never returned from California.

He stepped out into the courtyard, answered.

"Hello?"

"Arnab?"

A pause. Then:

"It's Shaun."

Old Voices, Old Ghosts

"Shaun?" Arnab said, blinking.

The voice was so familiar it scraped a nerve.

"I saw the article. So did the board. Listen, I won't take much of your time—we're stunned, man. I mean… this is bigger than tech. What you've done there…"

"It's just a pilot," Arnab said, soft.

"Don't downplay it. We've been talking since this morning. The way you've humanized a legacy system, built ground-up empathy into code…"

He paused.

"We need that here. *You.* We need you back."

Arnab leaned against a pillar, one leg folded casually, heart beating harder now.

The Offer

"Arnab, I've spoken to Vinny. The new CTO wants to restructure Global Field Solutions. They need someone who's lived it—who's proven they can align system logic with human reality. This is it, man. Your chance to head the team."

Arnab didn't speak.

"We're talking remote-first, open model, seven-figure retainer, travel covered, design authority. You name it."

More silence.

"Just say the word. We'll fly you out next week."

The Refusal

Arnab looked across the field.

Two boys were racing barefoot along the rail tracks.

Rajesh was teaching a new pensioner how to use the SMS balance checker.

Inside, his father was laughing over tea with a former courier from 1992.

He closed his eyes, then opened them with a smile.

"Shaun... I appreciate the offer. But I'm not coming back."

"Wait—what?"

"I found something here that I never found there."

Shaun was quiet. "What?"

Arnab's voice was peaceful now.

"Harmony."

"These imperfect systems... these files that smell of old ink... these people who remember birthdays without calendars... they taught me what peace is."

"And what love looks like when it's not wrapped in convenience."

Shaun didn't argue.

He couldn't.

Because there are some truths too whole to interrupt.

"Goodbye, my friend," Arnab said gently.

"Goodbye, Arnab. I hope we meet again—someday."

The Confession – Telling the Truth

It was nearly sunset.

The village sky had turned a muted gold, and the breeze carried that earthy scent of dust, mango blossoms, and home-cooked dal from nearby kitchens.

Arnab stepped through the courtyard gate slowly, as if his feet were measuring the weight of what he was about to do.

On the verandah, **his mother** sat on a low wooden bench, peeling pointed gourds for dinner. Her dupatta rested on her head, but strands of Gray had escaped the sides and framed her face in soft fatigue.

His father was near the edge of the courtyard, scanning a newspaper under the slanting light, nodding occasionally as he read.

They looked content.

Which made it harder.

But some truths are too heavy to carry alone. They must be set down—even if they shatter the silence.

The Opening Words

"Ma… Baba," he called softly.

Both looked up.

There was something in his voice that made them straighten.

Arnab stepped closer.

"Can we sit? I need to tell you something. Everything."

His mother immediately wiped her hands on the end of her sari and gestured toward the bench. His father folded the newspaper slowly, watching him.

Arnab sat.

And for the first time since his return to India…

He told them **everything**.

The Crash and the Darkness

"I was doing well in the U.S. You know that part."

They nodded.

"I had just been promoted. We were expecting a baby."

Seema gasped. Her eyes darted to Gourango's face.

"Her name was going to be **Rhea**, after her grandmother," Arnab whispered, smiling sadly.

He paused. The words were harder now.

"There was a party. The team was celebrating. Rhea was glowing. We were… happy."

He swallowed.

"That night… there was an accident. A car didn't stop at a signal."

His mother's hand flew to her mouth.

His father's jaw clenched.

"I survived. She didn't. Neither did the baby."

The Fallout

Silence.

Only the call of a distant koel.

"I lost everything in a night," Arnab continued. "And then… the company let me go. Said they had to cut costs. They gave my job to someone I'd once had to fire."

"I packed everything into three boxes. I flew back."

"I didn't tell you because I couldn't. Because saying it aloud would mean it was real."

He looked at them now—really looked.

"I came here because I didn't know where else to go."

A Storm Breaks, Quietly

Seema couldn't hold back her sobs anymore.

She reached forward and held Arnab's face in her hands like he was still ten years old and running home with scraped knees.

"You carried all of this… alone?" she wept.

Arnab's voice cracked. "I didn't know how not to."

Gourango stood. Pushed his chair aside.

Then sat down beside his son and pulled him into a strong, wordless hug.

He didn't say sorry.

He didn't say anything.

He just held him.

And in that space between them, **years of silence melted**.

The Embrace

The three of them—mother, father, son—sat there, huddled like survivors of a storm that had passed through quietly but left everything changed.

They cried.

Not out of pain.

But out of the **relief that comes when truth is finally spoken**.

And when it was done, when the tears had dried on Seema's cheeks, she looked at him and smiled.

The Final Line

She ran a hand over his hair, kissed his forehead, and whispered:

"Do not worry, Arnab. This is our world… and nothing wrong will happen to us."

The tears had dried on Seema's and Gourango's cheeks, but the warmth of the embrace lingered long after.

They sat like that for a while, a tangled circle of grief, love, and redemption.

Arnab felt something uncoil inside his chest—something that had been knotted tight for years.

He wasn't alone anymore.

He wasn't broken beyond repair.

Here, in this imperfect old house, in the arms of two imperfect but unconditional souls, he had found it: **Home.**

As they sat there, the night outside deepened into velvet.

And from somewhere across the village lanes, floating on the cold winter wind, a voice rose —

Cracked, weathered, but full of aching truth:

"Manush bhojle sonar manush pabi…"
(If you truly understand another human being,
you will find the Golden Man, the divine inside.)

The Baul singer's words drifted across the tiled roofs, seeped through the broken windows, and wrapped around them like a blessing.

Arnab closed his eyes.

And for the first time in many, many years—**he felt complete.**

Epilogue: Letters Never Die

Six months had passed.

The Ashapur Post Office now had two Wi-Fi routers, an AI-assisted routing algorithm, and a new counter labelled:

"Digital & Legacy Access – Ask Here."

But the most remarkable thing wasn't the hardware.

It was the foot traffic.

Villagers came not just to post parcels or collect pensions.
They came to read the archives — to see how their fathers, mothers, and grandparents were once lovingly recorded in thick brown registers, penned with fountain pens by a man they now called **"Sir Mentor."**

Gourango Chatterjee sat in his old chair, his title plate now polished and slightly larger.

He didn't handle transactions anymore.

He taught.

Two trainees sat beside him each day, learning how **memory could become architecture**, how **patterns led to answers**, and how **technology must begin with trust**.

Arnab's Routine

Every morning, **Arnab** walked to the post office with a satchel that held a laptop, a notebook, and a single photograph of **Rhea**, clipped to the first page.

He never missed a sunrise.

He never missed a tea break with his father.

He never once wished he was elsewhere.

Because **home had stopped being a place of escape.**

It had become a place of meaning.

New Roots: The Birth of a Dream

A few lanes away from the post office, beside the old banyan tree, another modest miracle had begun.

Arnab had opened a small NGO —
a learning center for children and the underprivileged, to teach them computers, English, life skills, and the art of dreaming bigger.

The name of the NGO was the name **he and Rhea had once chosen for their unborn child**:

"Ishaan Foundation."

Simple.
Unassuming.
But every wall, every chalkboard, every smile inside it carried **their shared dream forward**.

A life that wasn't lost—just reborn in a thousand little ways.

Rajesh's Letter

One afternoon, Rajesh came running into the post office.

"Dada, this came in today. No sender, but look—"

Arnab opened the envelope slowly.

Inside, a short note:

*"Dear Sir,
I came to visit Ashapur last week. You didn't see me.
But I saw everything.
You didn't fix a post office.
You redefined purpose.
Thank you.

— R."*

Arnab folded the letter gently.

Placed it in a drawer marked **"For Tomorrow's Archivists."**

And smiled.

Some doors you build.

Some doors you inherit.

And some… you unlock just by returning home.

Final Lines

In a small village, between fields and faith, between fathers and sons, between paper and pixels — a revolution had happened.

Quiet.

Patient.

Unshakeable.

Because sometimes, to move the world forward, you must first go back to where it began.

"Somewhere between old ink and new code, we found ourselves again."

About the Author

Prithwish Banerjee - An atomic soul with fusion of thoughts and fission of energy. A techie with some passion to think .